英語語法
從單字到句子

English Grammar

楊篳璐 著

不怕開口說英語！
用語法搭建橋梁，解決溝通難題

丟掉背誦公式、告別死記硬背
用邏輯搭建英文句子

突破語言運用瓶頸
語法學習不再枯燥！

目 錄

上篇：基礎句型 —— 掌握簡單句

一　語法的基本問題 …………………………006

二　簡單句的5種基本句型 …………………011

三　名詞類結構 ………………………………016

四　謂語動詞（一）：時態和語態 …………023

五　謂語動詞（二）：主謂一致 ……………033

六　謂語動詞（三）：語氣 …………………042

七　非謂語動詞（一）：動名詞 ……………050

八　非謂語動詞（二）：分詞 ………………055

九　非謂語動詞（三）：不定詞 ……………061

十　形容詞 ……………………………………067

十一　副詞 ……………………………………073

十二　介詞 ……………………………………079

中篇：進階句型 —— 解析複合句

一　名詞從句 ································· 090

二　形容詞從句 ····························· 096

三　副詞從句 ································· 104

四　對等從句 ································· 111

下篇：高階句型 —— 探索修辭變化

一　複句簡化 ································· 118

二　形容詞從句簡化 ······················ 123

三　名詞從句簡化 ························· 132

四　副詞從句簡化 ························· 138

五　複句簡化綜合 ························· 147

六　倒裝句 ···································· 154

參考書目

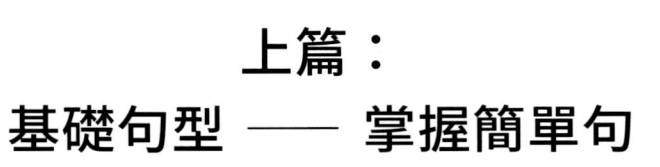

上篇：
基礎句型 —— 掌握簡單句

上篇：基礎句型─掌握簡單句

一　語法的基本問題

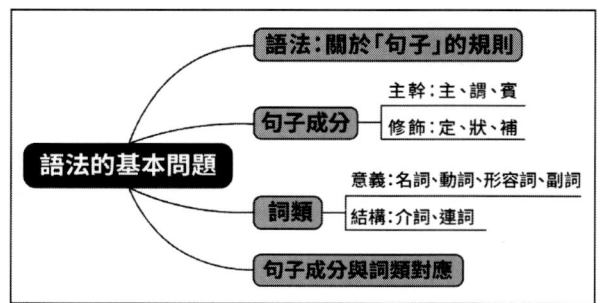

本節要點提示

- 什麼是語法？為什麼要學習語法？如何學習語法？
- 什麼是句子成分？句子都有哪些成分？
- 什麼是詞類？有哪些詞類？
- 詞類和句子成分的關係是什麼？

問題1　什麼是語法？語法就是關於「句子」的規則。

➡字母＋字母＝詞（構詞法）

➡詞＋詞＝句（語法）

➡句＋句＝篇章（章法）

一　語法的基本問題

問題2　為什麼學語法？

輸入：閱讀／聽力➡分析（解構）

輸出：寫作／口語➡累積（結構）

問題3　如何學語法？

不只記住「是什麼」，更要理解「為什麼」；「精通」語法體系；運用自如。

問題4　什麼是句子成分？

一個句子根據功能的不同，切分出的語言片段。

問題5　句子有哪些成分？

➡主幹：主、謂、賓

比如：

I swim.

I love you.

➡修飾：定、狀、補

比如：

I drink water. ➡ I drink hot water.（定語）

In winter, I only drink hot water.（狀語）

比如：

The food looks delicious.（主語補足語）

I think the gift too expensive.（賓語補足語）

問題 6　什麼是詞類？

根據句子的成分劃分，在句子中能夠充當相同成分，發揮相同功能的詞可以歸成同一類，稱為詞類。

問題 7　有哪些詞類？

➡意義：名詞、動詞、形容詞、副詞

➡結構：介詞、連詞

＊本書上篇對於每一詞類，都以相應章節具體介紹其語法功能；動詞語法要點最多，透過六節內容來介紹（其他詞類均為一節）；連詞與複合句關係密切，在本書中篇與複合句結合講解。

問題 8　詞類與句子成分關係？

主語←→名詞類

謂語←→動詞類

賓語←→名詞類

一　語法的基本問題

定語←→形容詞類

狀語←→副詞類

非主語／賓語←→介詞＋名詞類

標示從句←→連詞

根據名詞前有沒有介詞：沒有➡主語／賓語；有➡定／狀／補語。

在謂語動詞前或後：前➡主語；後➡賓語。（一般句型）

連詞與介詞的區別：介詞＋詞／詞組；連詞＋句子。

詞組和句子的區別：有謂語動詞就是句子；沒有就是詞組。

比如：

a new book in a small box on my desk（詞組）

Get out!（句子）

謂語動詞是句子的象徵。

* 一個句子必須要有謂語動詞；

*（除並列謂語外）一個句子只有一個謂語動詞；

* 有幾個謂語動詞就有幾個句子（從句）。

上篇：基礎句型—掌握簡單句

本節內容概要

1. 語法是關於句子內部的詞以及詞與詞之間關係的規則。
2. 根據在句子中發揮的功能不同，可以將句子拆分成 6 種成分。

   主幹 —— 主、謂、賓

   修飾 —— 定、狀、補

3. 根據能夠充當的句子成分不同，英語單字有 6 種主要詞類。

   實詞 —— 名詞、動詞、形容詞、副詞

   虛詞 —— 介詞、連詞

4. 英語句子必不可少的標示是謂語動詞；一個英語句子（包括從句）有且只有一個謂語動詞。

二　簡單句的 5 種基本句型

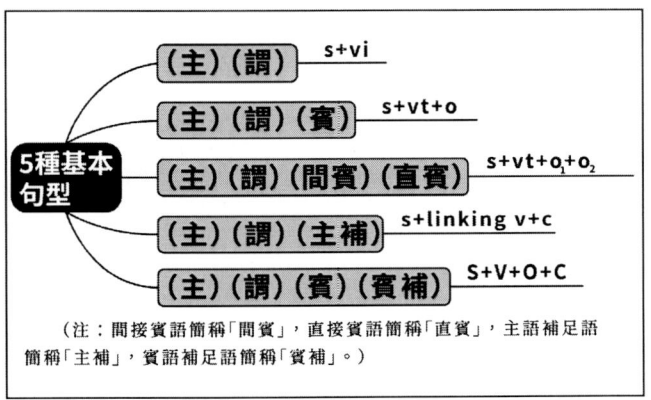

（注：間接賓語簡稱「間賓」，直接賓語簡稱「直賓」，主語補足語簡稱「主補」，賓語補足語簡稱「賓補」。）

本節要點提示

- 以「主語補足語」的概念替代「主繫表」結構的「表語」提法；與賓語補足語概念相互印證，語法系統會更簡明。

上篇：基礎句型—掌握簡單句

用公式表示的簡單句 5 種基本句型：

句型公式	字母含義	例句
s+vi	s:subject 主語 v:verb 謂語 vi: 不及物動詞 vt: 及物動詞 linking v: 繫動詞 o:object 賓語 c:complement 補語	His back aches.
s+vt+o		He hurts his back.
s+vt+o¹+o²		She gives me a cup.
s+linking v+c		She is nice.
s+v+o+c		I find him interesting.

句型 1　s+vi（主語＋不及物動詞）

不及物動詞 vi: 主語可以獨立發生的動作，不牽涉到別的人或物，後面不帶賓語。如 die（死亡）。

句型 2　s+vt+o（主語＋及物動詞＋賓語）

及物動詞 vt: 必須發生在另一個對象上的動作，後面必須帶賓語。如動詞 carry（搬運）的後面必須有一個東西「被搬運」。

句型 3　s+vt+o1+o2（主語＋「給」＋間接賓語「人」＋直接賓語「物」）

➡哪些動詞可以帶兩個賓語？

帶有「給」出意味的動詞。

They give me a cup.

They send me a cup.

They make me a cup.

They deliver me a cup.

They pass me a cup.

They leave me a cup.

They buy me a cup.

They throw me a cup.

She makes us a delicious meal.（「給」出一頓飯）

He sent me a birthday gift.（「給」出禮物）

The boy asks his mother many questions every day.（「給」出問題）

句型 4　s+linking v+c（主語＋「是」＋主語補足語）

例句	繫動詞及意義
The question seems difficult.	seem 似乎是
His demands appear reasonable.	appear 顯得是
The girl looks pretty.	look 看起來是
This movie sounds interesting.	sound 聽起來是
The drink tastes sweet.	taste 嚐起來是
Roses smell pleasant.	smell 聞起來是
I feel terrible.	feel 感覺是

She becomes my friend.	become 成為
The milk turns bad.	turn 轉變為
His words proved untrusted.	prove 證實為
Lily makes a good mother.	make 使成為

➡常見的連綴動詞（又稱「繫動詞」）有哪些？

除be動詞（包括am、is、are、was、were……）狀態繫動詞外，還有持續繫動詞、表象繫動詞、感官繫動詞、變化繫動詞和終止繫動詞。

➡可以作補語的詞類有哪些？

形容詞和名詞。

➡一個句子是不是「主補結構」？

檢驗技巧：主語是補語。

句型5　s+v+o+c

➡一個句子是不是「賓補結構」？

檢驗技巧：賓語是補語。

I find the book interesting.=The book is interesting.

I consider his demand acceptable.=His demand is acceptable.

He made me a good person.=I am a good person.

二 簡單句的 5 種基本句型

➡ 區分名詞作補語的「主謂賓補」結構和「雙賓結構」。

My father gives me a dog. ≠ I am a dog.

➡ be 動詞單獨使用時，含義為「存在」。

To be or not to be, that is the question.

生存還是死亡，那就是問題所在。

本節內容概要

1. 單句／複句／合句：只有「一套」謂語動詞的句子，就是單句；and、but、or 連接的兩個或多個並列動詞，按一套謂語算；謂語是動詞短語 have done、will do 等時，也按一套謂語算。
2. 謂語動詞陳述能力不同，產生了 5 種單句結構。

    主謂結構：謂語動詞能獨立完整敘事；

    主謂賓結構：謂語動詞要作用於賓語；

    雙賓結構：謂語動詞有「給」的意味；

    主補結構：謂語動詞有「是」的意味；

    賓補結構：謂語動詞有「覺得，使得……」的意味。

上篇：基礎句型—掌握簡單句

三　名詞類結構

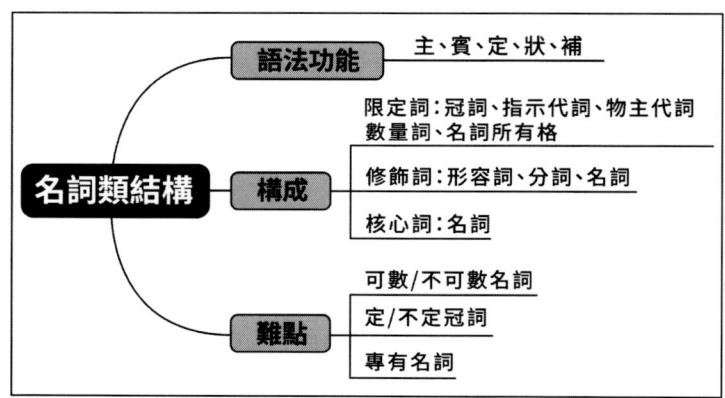

本節要點提示

・把名詞類結構看成一個由三部分組成的公式化結構，可以簡化很多「臨時」、「例外」的規則，尤其是對於冠詞的用法更容易理解。

問題1　名詞類結構在句子中可以作哪些語法成分？

➡除了謂語之外的所有成分：主、賓、定、狀、補。

問題 2　名詞類結構由哪幾個部分構成？

➡限定詞＋修飾詞＋核心詞

＊三個部分順序固定不變：

限定詞在開頭，修飾詞在中間，核心詞在結尾。比如：

a good person

the best answer

those happy kids

my special skill

many new friends

＊三個構成部分，每個都可以省略。

無限定詞：They are great people.

無修飾詞：I want an apple.

無核心詞：The young and the old are the same.

問題 3　限定詞的語法功能是什麼？有哪些種類？

➡限定詞是名詞的身分象徵：看到限定詞，說明其後必有名詞。

➡常見的限定詞有 5 種。

冠詞：the/a/an

指示代詞：this/that/these/those

形容詞性物主代詞：my/our/your/his/her/its/their

數量詞／數量短語：many/much/a little/a lot of

名詞所有格：n's/ns'

問題 4　名詞類結構中的修飾詞語法功能是什麼？有哪些種類？

➡說明名詞的屬性、特徵。

➡常見的修飾詞有三種。

形容詞：happy girls; nice tea

分詞：a swimming pool; a damaged car

名詞：a sports meeting; the students' book

問題 5　核心詞涉及哪些語法問題？

(1) 複數名詞的詞形變化。

可數名詞一般要在詞尾添加 -s 或 -es，也有少量不規則變化。

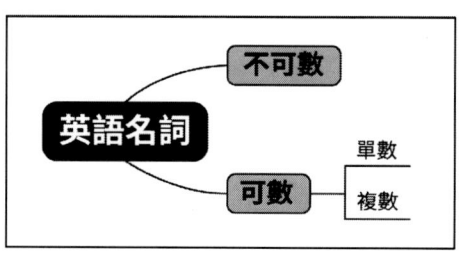

三　名詞類結構

(2) 名詞的單位。

→可數名詞不用量詞：數詞＋可數名詞

a cat; two dogs; three cows; four horses

→不可數名詞要用量詞：數詞＋量詞＋ of ＋不可數名詞

a cup of coffee; two cups of coffee

* 數詞＋修飾詞＋量詞＋ of ＋不可數名詞

a cup of nice coffee（X）

a nice cup of coffee（√）

問題 6　不定冠詞 a/an 涉及哪些語法規則？

(1) 單數可數名詞前，必須用不定冠詞 a/an。

I get a new book.

(2) 複數可數名詞前，不能用不定冠詞 a/an。

Free samples are everywhere in the supermarket.

(3) 抽象名詞前，不能用不定冠詞 a/an。

Diligence is not always effective.

(4) 物質名詞前，不能用不定冠詞 a/an。

We can't live without water and air.

問題 7　定冠詞 the 涉及哪些語法規則？

➡「特別指定」的名詞前要用 the。

I meet a girl.

I meet the girl you like.

Chinese food is my favorite.

The food made by my mother is my favorite.

A door of my house was broken.

The front door of my house was broken.

I'm going to school now.

There is a school nearby.

Do you mind if I take a seat?

Do you mind if I take the seat?

問題 8　什麼是專有名詞？
　　　　專有名詞前為什麼無須使用限定詞？

➡專有名詞：表達世界上「獨一無二」的人、事、物名稱的詞。書寫形式上，首字母大寫。

➡專有名詞前無須使用限定詞，也沒有複數形式。

a New York（X）

New Yorks（X）

the New York（X）

the New York people（√）

＊如何判定一個首字母大寫的名詞是不是專有名詞？

➡若擴大計算範圍，不再表達獨一無二的事物，就不是專有名詞。

比如：

I have a date on Sunday.

There are five Sundays this month.

Mr. Green is President of our school.

Mr. Green is a better President than Mr. White.

➡專有名詞實際上是名詞類結構中的修飾詞，而非核心詞時。

比如：the Pacific (Ocean) 太平洋

the Atlantic (Ocean) 大西洋

the Indian Ocean 印度洋

the Mediterranean (Sea) 地中海

the Dead (Sea) 死海

the Philippine Islands 菲律賓群島

the Alps Mountains 阿爾卑斯山

the Mississippi (River) 密西西比河

the Titanic (Ship)「鐵達尼號」郵輪

the Hilton (Hotel) 希爾頓酒店

the United Nations 聯合國

本節內容概要

1. 名詞類結構：

   限定詞＋修飾詞＋核心詞。

2. a/an ＝一個。

   複數名詞、不可數名詞、專有名詞不用 a/an。

3. 「特別指定」的名詞前要用 the。

四　謂語動詞（一）：時態和語態

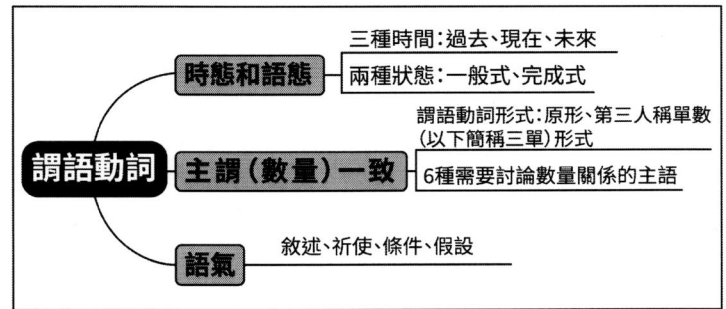

本節要點提示

* 在傳統語法講解中，英語謂語動詞有 16 種時態，每種時態又分主動和被動語態，這樣一共有 32 種構成樣式，看似繁瑣，卻有規律。其中大量重複的內容，就是可以整理、簡化的空間。
* 在傳統語法講解中，與各種時態搭配的時間狀語規則也很繁瑣，如何透過直觀的圖示來簡明呈現呢？

上篇：基礎句型—掌握簡單句

問題 1　英語動詞涉及多少種語法問題，如何歸類？

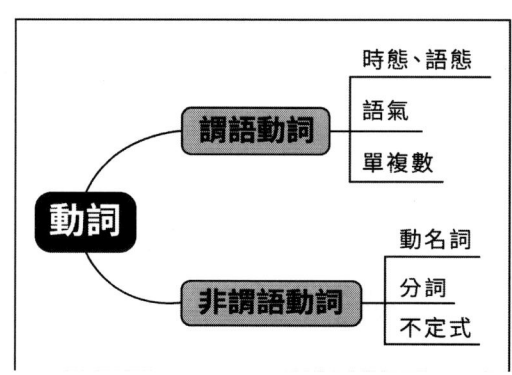

問題 2　傳統語法的時態是如何分類的？

➡ 16 種時態：

	一般	進行	完成	完成進行
過去	一般過去	過去進行	過去完成	過去 完成進行
現在	一般現在	現在進行	現在完成	現在 完成進行
將來	一般將來	將來進行	將來完成	將來 完成進行
過去 將來	一般 過去將來	過去將來 進行	過去將來 完成	過去將來 完成進行

四 謂語動詞（一）：時態和語態

➡ 32 種結構變化：

		過去	現在	將來	過去將來
一般	主動	Ved	V/Vs	will V	would V
	被動	was/were Ven	am/is/are Ven	will be Ven	would be Ven
完成	主動	had Ven	have/has Ven	will have Ven	would have Ven
	被動	had been Ven	have/has been Ven	will have been Ven	would have been Ven
進行	主動	was/were Ving	am/is/are Ving	will be Ving	would be Ving
	被動	was/were being Ven	am/is/are being Ven	will be being Ven	would be being Ven
完成進行	主動	had been Ving	have/has been Ving	will have been Ving	would have been Ving
	被動	had been being Ven	have/has been being Ven	will have been being Ven	would have been being Ven

注：V 代表動詞原形，Ved 代表動詞過去式，Ven 代表動詞過去分詞，Ving 代表動詞現在分詞。

➡總結整理：各種動詞時態含有的 4 種構成要素：

（1）be 動詞。

am, is, are, was, were, been, being

（2）助動詞。

have, has, had, haven, having; will, would

(3)分詞。

Ving, Ven

(4)一般實義動詞。

動詞原形,動詞第三人稱單數,動詞過去式

問題 3　重複出現的謂語構成要素,有什麼規律?

➡ 4 種要素有規律地重複出現:

被動語態一定包含:be, Ven;

進行時態一定包含:be, Ving;

完成時態一定包含:have, Ven。

在 32 種結構中,24 種都有 be 動詞。

➡這些要素重複出現,背後的本質規律在於:

be 動詞本身有含義:表示某種狀態。(be 的本義是存在)

分詞本身有含義:Ving 有「進行」意味;Ven 有「被動」意味。

助動詞 have 本身有含義:持續,完成。

助動詞 will 本身有含義:將發生,未發生。

總之,「時態」不是無意義的規則,而是有意義的表達,這些意義透過 be 動詞、分詞和助動詞本身自帶的含義來展現。

四　謂語動詞（一）：時態和語態

＊分詞不是謂語的構成部分。

傳統語法把「分詞」算作謂語的一部分，這是矛盾的，因為分詞是「非」謂語動詞，不能作謂語。

在「進行式」謂語 be+Ving，「被動式」謂語 be+Ven 中，真正的謂語只能是其中的 be 動詞。分詞語法功能相當於形容詞，所以實際上作的是「主語補足語」。

按單句的 5 種基本類型中的主補結構來理解，「時態」、「語態」都是分詞作補語所描述的主語「狀態」。

所以，當謂語動詞是一般實義動詞（原形 V、三單 V、過去式 V），不是 be 動詞或其他繫動詞時，就不是主補結構，其後不出現分詞，也就只有「一般」時態。

問題 4　「謂語動詞」時態系統如何簡化整理？

（1）關鍵在於傳統語法的時態／語態分類中，重複概率最高的 be 動詞（及繫動詞），應該和一般實義動詞一樣，看作是謂語。

（2）結合簡單句的 5 種基本句型，謂語動詞為 be 動詞時，對應句型 4，也就是 S+Linking V+C（主語＋謂語＋主語補足語）的結構；謂語動詞為一般實義動詞時，對應另外 4 種句型。

（3）在傳統語法時態分類中，進行時態的現在分詞和被動語態中的過去分詞，都不是謂語，而是主語補足語，所

以,進行時態和被動語態是分詞表達的意義,分詞的語法屬性等於形容詞,不應該在謂語動詞的語法中討論。

(4) 把 Ving 和 Ven 排除謂語討論範圍,謂語動詞的時態類型,就只有 6 種情況,而不是 32 種。

➡ 根據動作或狀態的開展方式,我們先將動詞分為「簡單式」和「完成式」,be 動詞和實義動詞都一樣:

簡單式:動作有始有終;形式為單獨的動詞。

完成式:動作無始有終;形式為 have+Ven。

➡ 表達者所處的時間點作為參照點「現在」,根據動作的起止點相對於參照點的位置,可以得出三種不同時間:「過去」、「現在」、「未來」。

➡ 簡單式和完成式都分別有三種動作發生的時間,所以英語謂語動詞的時態一共分為 6 種。

謂語動詞		過去時間	現在時間	將來時間
簡單式	be 動詞	was/were	am/is/are	will be
	實義動詞	Ved	V/Vs	will V

四　謂語動詞（一）：時態和語態

謂語動詞		過去時間	現在時間	將來時間
完成式	be 動詞	had been	have/has been	will have been
	實義動詞	had Ven	have/has Ven	will have Ven

＊由於情態動詞不能單獨使用，所以表示「將來」含義的 will 與其後的動詞原形，以及表示「持續／完成」含義的 have 與其後的過去分詞，要分別看成不可拆分、不可替換的整體，這和 be 動詞與其後的分詞可拆分替換的情況不同。

問題 5　如何以簡明圖示的方式呈現英語謂語動詞的 6 種時態？

（1）畫「時間軸」：一條從左到右的射線，代表時間從過去到未來的流動。

（2）確定「參照點」：說話者或者寫作者所處的時間即為核心參照點「現在」，在時間軸射線上以一個「小叉」號標記。

（3）「簡單式」動作時間：因為動作有始有終，所以可用括號標記。

（4）「完成式」動作時間：因為動作無始有終，所以只能用一個向上的豎箭頭標記動作結束點，配合一條向左無限延伸的虛線，表示起點不能確定。

➡「簡單式」謂語圖示及例句：

＊過去時間：小叉在括號右邊

- - - - (- - - -) - - - ✗ - - - - ▶

He established this company in 1990.（實義動詞：主／謂／賓）

I was doing my homework yesterday.（be 動詞：主／謂／主補）

They were questioned an hour ago.（be 動詞：主／謂／主補）

＊現在時間：小叉在括號裡面

- - - - (- - ✗ - -) - - - - ▶

He is the boss of this company now.（be 動詞：主／謂／主補）

Natural environment is being polluted.（be 動詞：主／謂／主補）

(- - - - ✗ - - - - ▶)

All mothers love their children.（實義動詞：主／謂／賓）

四 謂語動詞（一）：時態和語態

＊未來時間：小叉在括號左邊

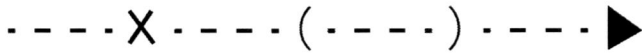

We will go on a trip in July.（實義動詞：主／謂）

➡「完成式」謂語圖示及例句：

＊過去時間：小叉在豎箭頭右邊

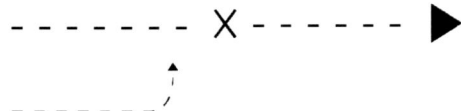

I had been smoking three packs of cigarettes a day before I decided to quit.（be 動詞：主／謂／主補）

＊現在時間：小叉在豎箭頭正上方

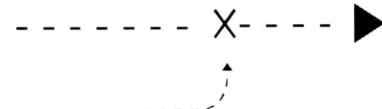

I have seen him.（實義動詞：主／謂／賓）

＊未來時間：小叉在豎箭頭左邊

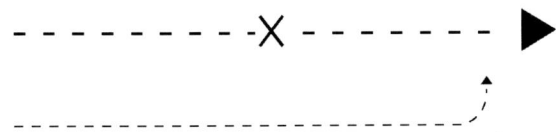

Next April, I will have worked here for 20 years.

031

上篇：基礎句型—掌握簡單句

本節內容概要

1. be 動詞和實義動詞才是謂語動詞，Ving 和 Ven 是分詞，分詞是「非」謂語動詞，「進行」只是 Ving 的詞義，「被動」是 Ven 的詞義，不能算作謂語語法範疇，「進行時」和「被動語態」被排除後，英語時態實際只有 6 種情況。
2. 助動詞 will、have 都不能單獨使用。will 與其後的動詞原形一起表示「未來發生」的含義，have 與其後的過去分詞一起表示「動作持續或完成」的含義，都是不可拆分替換的整體。
3. 動作開展方式，分為有始有終的「簡單式」和無始有終的「完成式」，根據動作發生的起／止點，與說話者所處時間點的比照關係，分為「過去」、「現在」和「未來」時間，就是判斷謂語動詞應該用哪種時態的依據，以圖示方式標記會更加直觀。

五　謂語動詞（二）：主謂一致

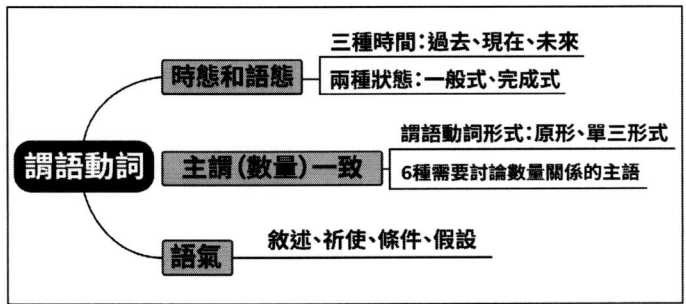

本節要點提示

※ 主謂一致，是指句子的主語和謂語在單複數方面的一致，而且只涉及謂語動詞的現在時態。過去時只涉及兩個動詞，也就是 be 動詞的 was 和 were 形式。

※ 主語單複數的判定，不用死記規則條目，而要結合語境去理解。

問題 1　主謂一致的語法規則是什麼？

➡現在時態的謂語動詞，分為原形和三單形式；當主語為第三人稱單數時，現在時謂語動詞要變為相應的三單形式，一般是在動詞末尾加 s 或者 es；主語為第一人稱、第二人稱或者複數時，現在時謂語動詞用原形。

➡簡言之，現在時謂語動詞的單複數形式，由主語單複數決定。

➡判斷主語是單數還是複數，要結合具體語境來分析，其中存在判斷困難的，可以整理為 6 種情況。

問題 2　存在判斷困難的 6 種主語分別如何構成？

(1)並列關係主語：多個人、事、物，常用 and 連接。

My sister Lily goes to Paris.

My sister and Lily go to Paris.

➡有限定詞時：主要看限定詞是一個還是多個。一個限定詞，則主語為單數，and 連接多個修飾詞，修飾同一個名詞；多個限定詞，則主語為複數，每一個限定詞標示出一個名詞，and 連接多個名詞。

The leader and instructor intends to speak to us.

The leader and the instructor intend to speak to us.

五 謂語動詞（二）：主謂一致

A cup and saucer is placed on the table.

A cup and a dish are placed on the table.

A brown and white dog attacks me.

A brown and a white dog attack me.

➡沒有限定詞時：看句子具體意思。

Bread and butter is not very tasty but very filling.

Bread and butter are both risen in price.

Oil and water do not mix.

(2)選擇關係主語：「就近一致」原則。

or、either...or、neither...nor 連接的兩部分是地位平等、任意選擇的關係，所以按與謂語動詞位置接近的一個判定。

The boys or the only girl is right.

Are the boys or the only girl right?

Either my father alone or both my parents are coming with me.

Either both my parents or my father alone is coming with me.

Neither he nor his friends were here yesterday.

Neither his friends nor he was here yesterday.

（3）排除關係主語：被否定、排除的部分不算主語，不考慮。

*but

Everyone but a few idiots is able to see this.

All but one of these apples are rotten.

*not、instead of、rather than、other than

Everyone, not you, understands the reason.

*not only... but also（不僅……而且）；not... but（不是……而是）

but 之後的名詞決定謂語動詞的單複數。

Not only you but also I am a student.

Not you but I am a student.

Not only I but also you are students.

Not I but you are students.

注意 but 的特殊含義：

*「除了」

Everybody but you is a student.

=Everybody except you is a student.

You are anything but a student.

=You are not a student.

五 謂語動詞（二）：主謂一致

* 與 not 等否定詞連用，表雙重否定，強調。

Nobody but likes the movie.

You are nothing but a student.

(4)修飾關係主語：看中心詞是單數還是複數。

* 比較狀語：as、than

I, as well as you, am surprised.

She, no less than you, is responsible for this job.

* 介詞短語

Mrs. Smith, with her 5 daughters, goes on a trip.

The use of computers in teaching now is popular.

主語：a ＋名詞＋ of 構成數量短語，後接可數名詞的複數。

謂語：就近一致。

There is a bag of apples.

This is a bag of apples.

A bag of apples are all rotten.

* 定語從句：關係詞作從句主語時，先行詞決定從句謂語單複數。

I don't trust those people who talk too much.

I don't trust that person who talks too much.

He has 3 ideas, which are equally good.

He has 3 ideas, which is a good start.

* 強調句型：It is/was+ 被強調部分 +that/who 從句。

that 從句謂語的單複數，取決於先行詞：

It is his 3 ideas that attract us.

(5)數量關係主語。

* 度量衡、時間、錢一律算單數。

10 hours is a long term.

2 kilograms is enough.

He makes $3,000 a week, which is a lot of money.

All the money has been spent.

* 凡搭配了 every 的都是單數。

Every student gets here on time!

Every boy and every girl does something for the group.

*each 是主語的一部分，謂語就用單數；each 不在主語位置，不影響判斷。

Each has 5 minutes to finish his speech.

Each of you has 5 minutes to finish your speech.

You have 5 minutes to finish your speech each.

五　謂語動詞（二）：主謂一致

*all、some、half、a lot of、the rest of：看整體意思。

All of these are rotten apples.

All of these is clean water.

Half of the apples are rotten.

Some of the money costs in traffic.

A lot of apples are rotten.

A lot of time has been wasted.

分析一個英語諺語：

All work and no play makes Jack a dull boy.

只會工作不玩耍，聰明孩子也變傻。

*none 作主語，謂語單複數皆可。

None of the apples is/are rotten.

特別注意兩個難點：

難點 1：

主語是 the number of+ 名詞：謂語用單數。

主語是 a number of+ 名詞：謂語用複數。

難點 2：

主語是 a pair of+ 名詞，情況複雜：

* 一個整體，不可分割的算單數。

A pair of trousers/pants is hanging there.

＊組合在一起用，但是分離的兩個個體的算複數。

A pair of shoes/rackets are given to me as a birthday gift.

＊似乎是一個整體，但著眼點是個體的算複數。

A pair of sunglasses make me look cool.

（6）s 結尾的名詞作主語。

＊不以 s 結尾，但實際可能表達複數含義的：集合名詞，比如 family 家人、crew 全體成員、faculty 全體教員、police 警察、committee 委員（會）等。

The committee are having a meeting now.

The committee is/are studying the proposal.

The committee is/are 75 years old.

The committee are 5 years old.

＊以 s 結尾，但是單數的名詞，如學科、疾病等。

Mathematics is not easy.

Statistics plays an important part in economics.

主語	標示詞	判斷依據
並列關係	and	限定詞
選擇關係	or either...or neither...nor	就近一致

五　謂語動詞（二）：主謂一致

主語	標示詞	判斷依據
排除關係	but not、instead of、rather than not…only、but also	不管，否定
修飾關係	比較 as、than 介詞（包括 except、besides） 關係詞	中心詞
數量關係	every、each all、some、half rest、none a pair of、a lot of 度量衡、時間、錢	可數／不可數
名詞詞尾	不以 s 結尾的複數—集合名詞 以 s 結尾的單數—學科、疾病	整體／個體

1. 主謂一致：一般現在時的謂語動詞的單複數，要與主語的單複數保持一致。單數動詞詞尾加 s 或 es，複數動詞用原形。

2. 主語的本質內容是什麼，才是決定謂語單複數的根本。

上篇：基礎句型—掌握簡單句

六　謂語動詞（三）：語氣

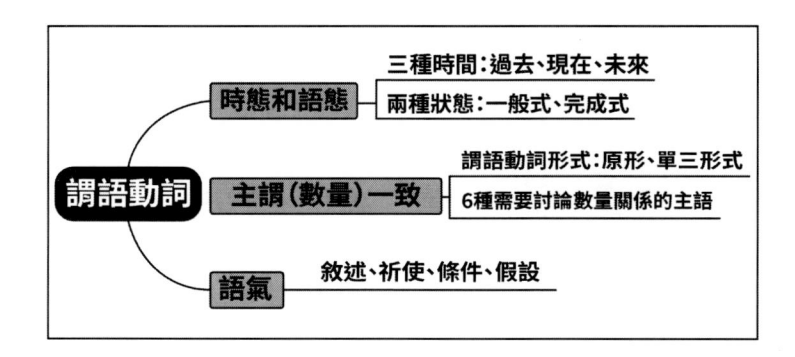

```
                         ┌─ 三種時間：過去、現在、未來
            ┌─ 時態和語態 ─┤
            │             └─ 兩種狀態：一般式、完成式
            │
            │                 ┌─ 謂語動詞形式：原形、單三形式
  謂語動詞 ─┼─ 主謂（數量）一致 ┤
            │                 └─ 6種需要討論數量關係的主語
            │
            └─ 語氣 ────── 敘述、祈使、條件、假設
```

本節要點提示

- 情態動詞表達主觀觀點，而非客觀事實；情態動詞的現在式和過去式，can/could，will/would，區別不在於時間，而在於可能性的大小。

- 條件語氣必須要有一個「條件從句」；若條件從句的謂語動詞用現在式，主句謂語動詞則用 will+ 動詞原形；若條件從句的謂語動詞用過去式，主句謂語動詞則用 would+ 動詞原形。

- 假設語氣的謂語動詞一律要往「過去」後推一個時間檔，以表明動作沒有真實發生。

六　謂語動詞（三）：語氣

問題1　謂語動詞有哪4種語氣？

敘述：所說的是真的；

祈使：希望能成真，但尚未實現；

條件：真假還不能確定；

假設：所說的與真實情況相反。

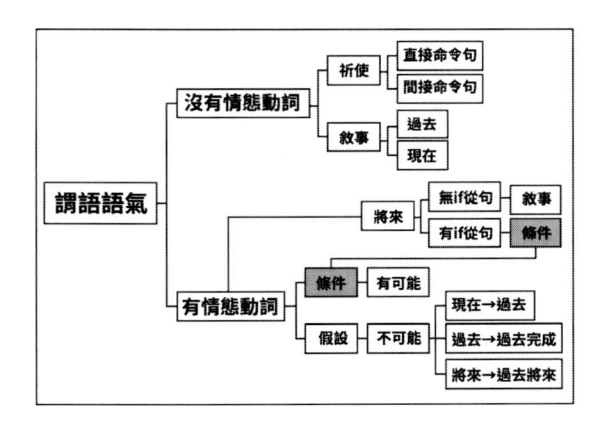

```
謂語語氣
├─ 沒有情態動詞
│    ├─ 祈使 ─┬─ 直接命令句
│    │        └─ 間接命令句
│    └─ 敘事 ─┬─ 過去
│             └─ 現在
└─ 有情態動詞
     ├─ 將來 ─┬─ 無if從句 ── 敘事
     │        └─ 有if從句 ── 條件
     ├─ 條件 ── 有可能
     └─ 假設 ── 不可能 ─┬─ 現在→過去
                        ├─ 過去→過去完成
                        └─ 將來→過去將來
```

問題2　假設語氣與情態動詞有什麼關係？

➡絕大多數的假設語氣都是透過情態動詞來展現的。

＊無情態動詞：相對真實的敘事和祈使語氣。

＊有情態動詞：相對虛擬的條件和假設語氣。

＊「現在式」情態動詞（can/will/shall/may）：條件語氣。

＊「過去式」情態動詞（could/would/should/might）：假設語氣。

問題 3　假設語氣的謂語動詞如何構成？

沒有發生過或不可能發生的事情：謂語動詞都相對推後一個時間。

＊對現在的假設，用動詞過去式來表達；

It is the time you were in bed now.

＊對過去的假設，用動詞過去完成式來表達；

If only I had arrived there then!

＊對將來的假設，用過去將來式來表達；

比較「條件」語氣，和「假設」語氣：

If I take the money, I will keep the secret for you.

If I should take the money, I would keep the secret for you.

翻譯成中文的假設語氣用「本來」、「要是」、「萬一」等語氣詞。

問題 4　直接祈使句如何構成？

➡主語：省略不說的第二人稱「你」和「你們」。

➡謂語：馬上就要發生的動作，雖未發生，但說話者主觀上認為「確定」，無須用情態動詞，直接用動詞原形。

Come in! Get out!

六　謂語動詞（三）：語氣

問題 5　間接祈使句如何構成？

➡間接祈使句／命令句：主句謂語動詞為「命令」、「要求」、「建議」，後接的賓語從句，都屬於間接祈使句／命令句。

The judge demands that the witness leave the courtroom.

➡間接祈使句謂語動詞，與一般的祈使句一樣，一律用動詞原形。

I insist that she go home now.

I suggest that she go home now.

I order that she go home now.

I expect that she go home now.

＊間接命令句的變體：

"It is + adj.+that…"，其中的形容詞如果有必須、應該等與命令要求等動作相關的意思，從句也屬於間接命令句。用形式主語 it 是因為發出命令的一方不具體。

It is necessary that she go home now!

It is advisable that she go home now!

問題 6　什麼是敘述語氣？

➡謂語動詞發生的時間：

過去：已發生，既成事實。

現在：正在發生的事實。

將來：未發生，但說話者主觀上明確認為會發生。

I went shopping yesterday.

I am walking into a shopping mall.

I will go shopping tomorrow.

自然規律，或者必定、馬上會發生的事情，可以不用情態動詞 will。

The weatherman says sunrise tomorrow is at 5:32.

The movie starts in 5 minutes.

問題 7　條件語氣如何構成？

➡有 if 的從句表示條件。條件語氣與陳述語氣的區別，在於有沒有 if 引導的條件從句；

說話者對於條件或時間這一部分，已認定為真實，不存在「不確定」的意味，所以從句中不使用情態動詞。

If he is late, I will go alone.

六 謂語動詞（三）：語氣

➡主句謂語中有情態動詞 will 或 would 表示「不確定」。條件語氣與假設語氣的區別，在於謂語動詞時間不推後，發生的可能性大於假設語氣。

*if 可以替換為其他功能相似的引導詞：

I will be ready when he comes.

*will/would 可以替換為其他情態動詞：

must, shall/should, can/could, may/might 等。

You are right.（事實）

You might be right.（不確定）

* 情態動詞的「過去」問題：

一方面，shall/should, will/would, can/could, may/might 不是現在式 / 過去式，而是可能性程度不同。

Can I help you?（雖然還未幫助，但我確定自己能幫助你）

Could you help me?（還未幫助，但我也不確定對方能否幫助我）

另一方面，情態動詞的過去式要借助 have+Ven 實現。

It may rain any minute now.

It may have rained last night.

問題 8　什麼是假設語氣？

➡假設語氣也叫「說反話」的語氣。

＊假設語氣與條件語氣的區別：

	條件語氣	假設語氣
發生可能性	不確定，有可能	與事實相反，不可能
謂語時間	不推後	現在➡過去 過去➡過去完成 將來➡過去將來
條件從句	必須有	可有可無

＊無論有沒有條件從句，從謂語的時間形式就足以辨析假設語氣：

沒有條件從句時：I wish I had more time.

有條件從句時：If I were you, I wouldn't do it.

有條件從句的假設語氣：從、主句的謂語動詞時間都後推一檔。

條件句：從句謂語用現在式，主句情態動詞用 will；

假設句：從句謂語用過去式，主句情態動詞用 would。

＊假設語氣的主句和從句發生的時間不統一，可能一個是過去，一個是現在：

If I had tried harder last year, I might be in Harvard right now.

六　謂語動詞（三）：語氣

本節內容概要

　　英語謂語動詞，根據說話者主觀感覺其所述的事情發生可能性大小，依次分為：祈使（必須發生）＞敘事（事實發生）＞條件（可能發生）＞假設（與事實相反，不可能發生）4 種語氣。

　　祈使語氣：分單句形式的直接命令句和賓語從句形式的間接命令句，謂語動詞都用動詞原形。

　　敘事語氣：根據事情發生的具體時間，謂語動詞分過去式和現在式，但一般不使用情態動詞。

　　條件語氣：需要有謂語為現在式的條件從句和包括一個情態動詞的主句，討論可能性。

　　假設語氣：謂語需要有情態動詞，而且是 would、could、should、might 等表示可能性較低的情態動詞。為了表明所說的事情不是真實發生的，謂語動詞時間還要後推一個檔，用過去表示現在、過去完成表示過去，以便區分。

049

上篇：基礎句型─掌握簡單句

七　非謂語動詞（一）：動名詞

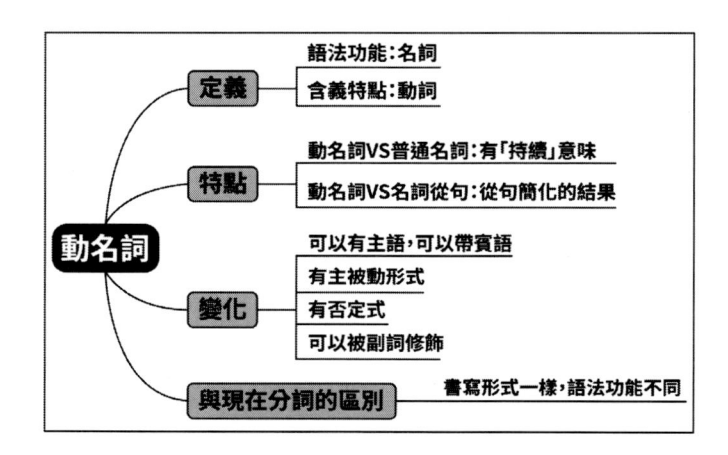

```
                ┌─ 定義 ─┬─ 語法功能：名詞
                │        └─ 含義特點：動詞
                │
                ├─ 特點 ─┬─ 動名詞VS普通名詞：有「持續」意味
                │        └─ 動名詞VS名詞從句：從句簡化的結果
    動名詞 ─────┤
                ├─ 變化 ─┬─ 可以有主語，可以帶賓語
                │        ├─ 有主被動形式
                │        ├─ 有否定式
                │        └─ 可以被副詞修飾
                │
                └─ 與現在分詞的區別 ── 書寫形式一樣，語法功能不同
```

本節要點提示

- 動名詞與名詞從句之間的關係：動名詞是名詞從句簡化的結果。從句簡化是本書下篇「高級句型」部分將要講解的主要內容。

- 透過本節內容學習，搞清楚為什麼有必要將書寫形式都是 Ving 的動名詞和現在分詞明確區分開來。

七　非謂語動詞（一）：動名詞

動詞的 6 種語法問題：

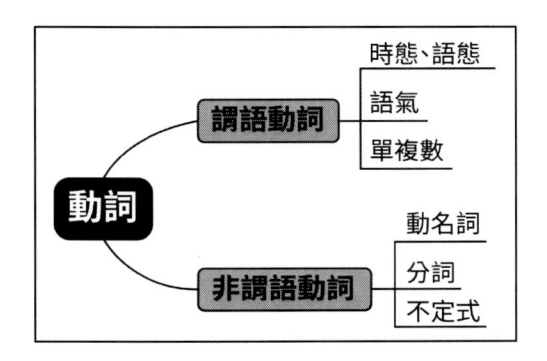

```
                    ┌── 時態、語態
         謂語動詞 ───┼── 語氣
         │          └── 單複數
動詞 ─────┤
         │          ┌── 動名詞
         非謂語動詞 ─┼── 分詞
                    └── 不定式
```

問題 1　什麼是動名詞？

➡動名詞：有動詞的含義和屬性，名詞的語法功能的動詞 ing 形式。

問題 2　動名詞有什麼特點？

➡動名詞 VS 普通名詞

普通名詞：表示「人、事、物」的名稱。

動名詞：表示動作習慣，有「持續」意味。

Let's get a drink.（酒精飲料）

Drinking is not a good habit.（飲酒的行為）

後綴為 -ion, -ance, -th 的普通名詞：「事情」、「動作」、「屬性」。與動名詞的區別：是否「持續」。

I am not afraid of death, but I am scared of dying.

➡動名詞的「數」。

There are two weddings at the restaurant tonight.

➡動名詞 VS 名詞從句

「從句簡化」的結果可能是動名詞結構。

I enjoy that I teach English on the Internet.

I enjoy teaching English on the Internet.

問題 3　動名詞可以有哪些變化？

動詞基本屬性：有動作的發出者（主語）；可以帶賓語；有主被動形式的變化；有否定式；可以被副詞修飾。

動名詞保留了動詞的這些屬性：

➡主謂結構轉化成動名詞短語。

I don't like that my boyfriend plays video games all day.

I don't like playing video games all day.（X）

I don't like my boyfriend's playing video games all day.（√）

➡動賓結構轉化成動名詞短語

Playing football is fun.

The playing of football is fun.

Football-playing is fun.

052

七　非謂語動詞（一）：動名詞

➡動名詞的被動式：Being+Ven

That I was invited here is a great honor.

Being invited here is a great honor.

➡動名詞的否定式：not+Ving

I apologize for my not being able to attend the meeting.

➡形容詞或副詞修飾動名詞：adj.+Ving; Ving+adv.

Heavy smoking can cause lung cancer.(adj.+n.)

Smoking heavily can cause lung cancer.(v.+adv.)

Even smoking once in a while can be harmful to one's lung.

They are hard working people.(adv.+adj.；現在分詞＝adj.)

問題 4　動名詞與現在分詞有什麼區別？

書寫一樣都是 Ving 的動名詞和現在分詞的區別在於：

➡在句子中所作的語法成分不同。

＊動名詞＝名詞：作主語、賓語及放在介詞之後。

This is a swimming suit.

I am swimming.

I teach him swimming.

I found a strange stone in the river, while swimming there.

上篇：基礎句型—掌握簡單句

＊現在分詞＝形容詞：作前置定語、補語及狀語（分詞短語）。

This is a swimming suit.

I am swimming.

I made him swimming.

I found a strange stone in the river, while swimming there.

動名詞和現在分詞雖然書寫形式一樣，但是語法功能完全不同，區分清楚才能保持整個語法系統上下貫通一致。

本節內容概要

1. 動名詞有動詞的含義和屬性，有名詞的語法功能。
2. 動名詞是「持續」的「動作過程」，是動態的；名詞是人、事、物的名稱，是靜態的。
3. 雖然書寫形式一樣，但動名詞語法功能相當於名詞；現在分詞語法功能相當於形容詞，有必要區分清楚。

八　非謂語動詞（二）：分詞

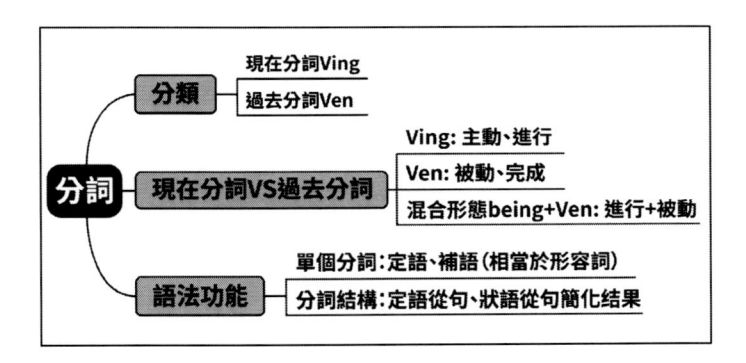

```
分詞 ┬─ 分類 ┬─ 現在分詞Ving
     │        └─ 過去分詞Ven
     │
     ├─ 現在分詞VS過去分詞 ┬─ Ving: 主動、進行
     │                      ├─ Ven: 被動、完成
     │                      └─ 混合形態being+Ven: 進行+被動
     │
     └─ 語法功能 ┬─ 單個分詞:定語、補語（相當於形容詞）
                 └─ 分詞結構:定語從句、狀語從句簡化結果
```

本節要點提示

- be 動詞與被動含義有關係嗎？
- 「謂語動詞被動語態」、「獨立主格」、「分詞構句」等語法概念有必要存在嗎？

上篇：基礎句型─掌握簡單句

問題 1　分詞如何分類，有什麼語法功能？

➡ 分詞分為：現在分詞 Ving 和過去分詞 Ven

分詞的語法功能：單個分詞作定語、補語，分詞結構用於簡化定語從句和狀語從句。

問題 2　分詞和形容詞有什麼關係？

分詞的語法功能相當於形容詞：用作定語、補語。

* 現在分詞 ── 形容詞：

That pretty girl runs away.（定語）

That smiling girl runs away.（定語）

That girl is pretty.（補語）

That girl is smiling.（補語）

* 過去分詞 ── 形容詞：

You should drink clean water.（定語）

You should drink boiled water.（定語）

The water is clean.（補語）

The water is boiled.（補語）

問題 3　過去分詞有什麼特殊含義？

➡過去分詞本身就表示「被動」，所以 be 動詞與「被動」含義無關。沒有 be 動詞，單獨過去分詞也可表達「被動」含義；be 動詞搭配 Ving 可以表達「進行」意味；其他繫動詞 +Ven 也可構成被動語態。比如：get praised; become irritated。

所以：be 動詞只是語法標示，無具體意義；be 動詞後作補語的名詞/形容詞/現在分詞/過去分詞才是表達具體意義的。

➡「被動」是 Ven 的屬性，與 be 動詞無關。

比如：Fallen leaves cover the street.（已經凋落）

I am done with you.（已經結束）

問題 4　現在分詞與過去分詞有什麼區別？

現在分詞：「主動」、「進行」；過去分詞：「被動」、「完成」。

➡表示「感覺」的動詞＋現在分詞與＋過去分詞，意義和用法有明顯的區別。

常見表示感覺的動詞：interest, excite, please, satisfy, surprise, amaze, scare, terrify, tire, exhaust, disappoint...

現在分詞:「令人……的」,多用於事物;過去分詞:「感到……的」,多用於人。

All the interested students can join the game.(感興趣的)

All the students can join the interesting game.(有趣的)

The students are interested.(感興趣的)

The game is interesting.(有趣的)

➡快速分辨及物／不及物動詞:

* 不及物動詞不帶賓語,沒有被動式。

* 動詞詞根＋詞綴構成的多音節動詞:及物與否由詞根決定。

比如:-sist「站」不及物➡ consist「組合」不及物

Water consists of hydrogen and oxygen.

Hydrogen and oxygen consist in water.

-pose「擺放」及物➡ compose「組合」及物

Hydrogen and oxygen compose water.

Water is composed of hydrogen and oxygen.

問題 5　如何同時表達「進行」和「被動」雙重含義?

➡使用現在分詞和過去分詞的混合形式:being+Ven

Those diamonds are being displayed for charity sale.

問題6　分詞結構能簡化哪些從句？

➡定語從句：

定語從句語法功能相當於形容詞。

定語從句可以刪除連接詞和主語，簡化為分詞結構作後置定語。

Products which are made in China are sold all over the world.

Products made in China are sold all over the world.

People who live in China have more chances to make money.

People living in China have more chances to make money.

➡狀語從句：

「獨立主格」、「分詞構句」這些提法是不合理的。

狀語從句語法功能相當於副詞。

狀語從句可以簡化為分詞結構作狀語，連詞有時不能刪。

Because / After he was wounded in war, the soldier was sent home.

Wounded in war, the soldier was sent home.

The factory produces things under unqualified condition, so

that they cause serious pollution.

The factory produces things under unqualified condition, causing serious pollution.

本節內容概要

1. 分詞意義是動詞，功能是形容詞；可用作定語／補語／狀語。
2. 現在分詞表「主動」、「進行」；過去分詞表「被動」和「完成」。
3. 定語從句簡化為分詞結構作定語；狀語從句簡化為分詞結構作狀語。

九　非謂語動詞（三）：不定詞

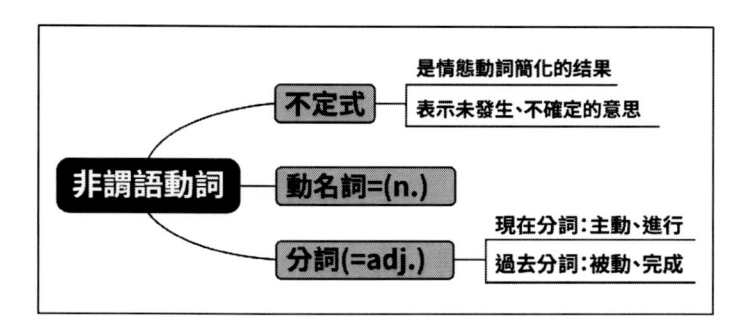

```
                        ┌─ 是情態動詞簡化的結果
             ┌─ 不定式 ──┤
             │           └─ 表示未發生、不確定的意思
非謂語動詞 ──┼─ 動名詞=(n.)
             │                     ┌─ 現在分詞：主動、進行
             └─ 分詞(=adj.) ────────┤
                                   └─ 過去分詞：被動、完成
```

本節要點提示

- 不定詞理解的關鍵在於「不定」兩個字，包含兩層意思：
  (1) 充當不固定的成分；(2) 表達不確定的語氣。

問題 1　不定詞和情態動詞有什麼關係？

➡都接動詞原形：

I can swim. ←→ I am able to swim.

She will go. ←→ She is likely to go.

➡都有「不確定」的意味：

061

She is right.（肯定）

She may be right.（不確定）

She seems to be right.（不確定）

➡都是未成事實：

He got the job.（已成事實）

He will get the job.（未成事實）

He is able to get the job.（可能性，非事實）

➡都沒有過去式，靠助動詞 have 表過去：

* 不定詞 to + 動詞原形，沒有過去式形態變化。

* 情態動詞 could、might 和 should 不是過去式，而是更不確定。

Could you help me?（眼前委婉請求）

It might rain.（眼前的推測）

* 過去的不確定語氣：情態動詞／to+have+Ven

It must have rained last night.

It seems to have rained last night.

➡所有重要的情態動詞，都有一個含義相當的不定詞結構：

must=have to

should=ought to

九　非謂語動詞（三）：不定詞

will/would=be going to

can/could=be able to

may/might=be likely to

問題 2　含有情態動詞的從句如何簡化為不定詞結構？

➡謂語部分含有情態動詞的從句，在簡化時：

＊情態動詞不能保留：句子／短語的關鍵區別是「謂語動詞」。

＊情態動詞不能刪除：不確定／確定的語氣含義不同。

➡所以從句情態動詞，只能簡化成短語中的不定詞：

＊謂語變為了非謂語：從句簡化成短語。

＊保留不確定含義：不定詞也表示「不確定」、「未發生」。

問題 3　不定詞結構的語法功能是什麼？

➡不定詞可以充當除謂語之外的所有成分。

＊不定詞符號 to 和情態動詞一樣，都是「額外添加」的，所以，它們不能單獨出現，一定要搭配動詞原形使用。

＊不定詞和情態動詞後的動詞原形都能再變換形式。

如：to V ➡ to be V-ed（未發生，被動）

can V ➡ can be V-ed（未發生，被動）

問題 4　不定詞與動名詞有什麼關係？

➡不定詞：不確定和未發生的事；動名詞：確定和已發生的事。

＊表示客觀行為的動詞：

I remember checking our luggage yesterday.（已做）

Please remember to check our luggage again tomorrow.（未做）

I forget checking our luggage yesterday.（已做）

I forgot to check our luggage yesterday.（未做）

Don't forget to check our luggage again tomorrow.（未做）

The speaker stops talking.（進行中）

The speaker stops to drink some water.（將要做，還未做）

＊表示主觀意願的動詞：

We plan to go on a trip.（未發生）

I avoid making the same mistake twice.（已發生）

I like/would like to go with you.（未發生）

I hate to say this, but I think you are mistaken.（將發生）

I try to get there on time.（未必做到）

I try being late for one time.（已經做到）

九　非謂語動詞（三）：不定詞

問題 5　什麼是「不帶 to 的不定詞」？

➡ to 是不定詞的象徵和根本，沒有 to 就不是不定詞了。

一般語法規則規定：make、have、let 等使役動詞和 see、hear、feel 等感官動詞後面要接「不帶 to 的不定詞」。這和上句的說法自相矛盾。

* 使役動詞：

They ask me to join the party.（要不要參加）

They make me join the party.（參加了）

* 感官動詞：

I hear her cry out loud.（叫了一聲）

I hear her crying.（持續在哭）

因為不持續發生的動作，不用現在分詞；非被動的動作，不用過去分詞；已發生，不用不定詞，所以只能用動詞原形。

➡謂語如果是：be+ 使役／感官動詞 -ed，主補結構。

謂語 be 不再有這些限制，所以不定詞符號 to 仍要出現。

I am made to join the party.

She is heard to cry out loud.

上篇：基礎句型—掌握簡單句

本節內容概要

1. 不定詞是含有情態動詞的從句簡化的結果，不定詞和情態動詞都表示「未發生」、「不確定」的意味。
2. 不定詞可以在句子中充當除了謂語之外的一切句子成分。

十　形容詞

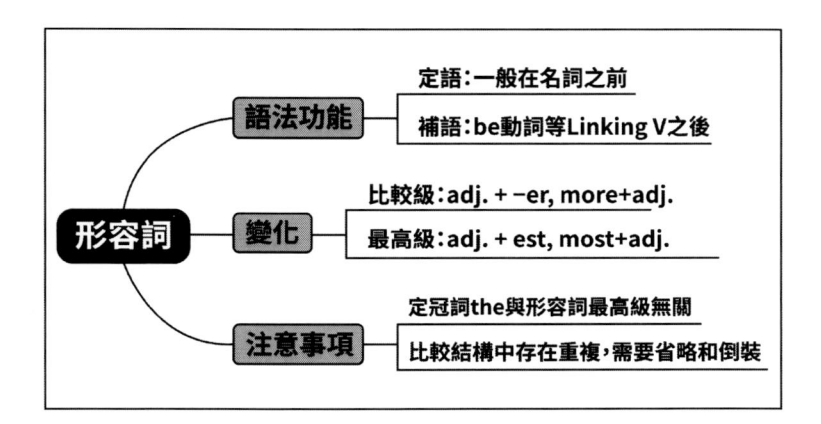

```
形容詞
├─ 語法功能
│   ├─ 定語：一般在名詞之前
│   └─ 補語：be動詞等Linking V之後
├─ 變化
│   ├─ 比較級：adj. + -er, more+adj.
│   └─ 最高級：adj. + est, most+adj.
└─ 注意事項
    ├─ 定冠詞the與形容詞最高級無關
    └─ 比較結構中存在重複，需要省略和倒裝
```

本節要點提示

- 作為前置定語的形容詞與作為補語的形容詞有何區別？
- 有比較關係的從句為何要倒裝？

問題1　形容詞的語法功能是什麼？

➡用作前置定語修飾名詞；用作補語（包括主補和賓補）。

問題 2　用作前置定語的形容詞在句子中處於什麼位置？

定語形容詞 attributive adjectives：描述核心名詞屬性。

→一般位置：名詞前

→特殊位置：名詞後

* 核心名詞是 someone、anybody 等時：

I get <u>something better</u>.

I don't believe <u>anybody else</u>.

* 部分以 a- 作前綴的形容詞：

<u>Money alone</u> can't get rid of our trouble.

You and your <u>sister alike</u> are welcome.

問題 3　名詞什麼時候可以用作前置定語？

→構成固定搭配：

movie theaters; a pencil box; these department stores

→以連字符號連接的複合結構作為修飾詞時，其中名詞沒有複數：

a five-year-old boy; a million-dollar bill

→名詞混搭其他詞類，也可以構成複合修飾詞：

an interest-oriented policy; a turn-of-the-century book

十　形容詞

問題 4　多個形容詞作前置定語，順序應該如何安排？

➡越不可變的、客觀的特質越靠近核心名詞；

越可變的、臨時的、主觀的屬性越遠離核心名詞。

two beautiful young American white girls

問題 5　用作補語的形容詞和用作定語的形容詞有何不同？

補語形容詞：predicate adjectives

➡功能上：補語形容詞是對名詞的臨時性、補充性說明；而定語形容詞則是對名詞屬性界定。

John is sick today.

John is a sick man.

➡形式上：補語形容詞可與其他詞組成短語，定語形容詞則不可以，需要用連字符號連接。

Chinese culture is 5,000 years old.

Chinese 5,000-year-old culture

➡含前綴 a- 的形容詞，更多用作補語；用作定語時要置於名詞後。

The man is still alive.

Coffee kept me awake all night.

問題 6　什麼是比較邏輯關係？

➡比較邏輯：「大於、小於、等於」。

A is <u>more</u> difficult than B.（大於）

A is <u>less</u> difficult than B.（小於）

A is <u>as</u> difficult as B.（等於）

問題 7　形容詞比較級和最高級有什麼變化規則？

➡單音節形容詞：詞尾加 -er/-est（除 good-better-best、bad-worse-worst、little-less-least、many/much-more-most 外）；

➡多音節形容詞：前加 more/most;

➡雙音節形容詞：看形容詞後綴。

*-ing、-ed、-ful、-less、-ous、-ive: 前加 more/most

famous —— more famous —— most famous

* 其他：詞尾加 -er、-est，或者前加 more、most 都可。

often —— oftener/more often

* 輔音字母 +y 結尾的形容詞：變 y 為 i+er/est

問題 8　形容詞最高級與定冠詞 the 有什麼關係？

➡定冠詞 the 屬於名詞類結構中的組成部分，與形容詞的變化無關。

十　形容詞

＊作為修飾詞的形容詞最高級前，才用 the；

注意核心名詞省略的情況：

You are the best.=You are the best one.

＊用作修飾詞的形容詞比較級前，也可以用 the：

Jack is the thinner of the twins.

＊用作補語的形容詞比較級和最高級前都不用 the：

The weather is good.

The weather is best here in July.

問題 9　什麼情況下，比較句型需要省略和倒裝？

➡比較結構中常出現重複的兩部分，為了句子簡練工整，重複部分要省略或倒裝。

➡重複名詞：可以用代詞代替，或者刪除。

＊形容詞性物主代詞＋名詞：用名詞性物主代詞代替。

My computer is more expensive than your computer.

My computer is more expensive than you.（X）

My computer is more expensive than yours.（√）

＊有修飾語的名詞類結構：用 that/those ＋修飾語代替。

The shoes made in China are better than those made in Japan.

上篇：基礎句型—掌握簡單句

➡重複謂語動詞：用助動詞 do/does/did 代替，並將之置於比較從句主語前。

倒裝的功能：突出比較的焦點，避免歧義。

Girls love cats more than boys.（X）

Girls love cats more than do boys.（√）

本節內容概要

1. 單個的形容詞在句中作修飾語／補語。
2. 形容詞比較級和最高級，要注意 the 的用法；注意比較句型中的省略和倒裝。

十一　副詞

```
副詞 ─┬─ 語法功能 ── 修飾除名詞外的其他成分
      │
      ├─ 種類 ──┬─ 強調語氣類副詞
      │         ├─ 方法狀態類副詞
      │         └─ 修飾句子類副詞
      │
      └─ 在句子中的位置 ── 一般比較靈活，但不完全任意
```

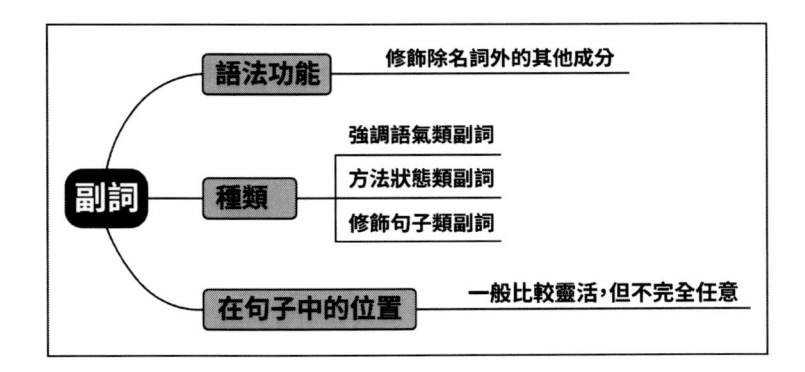

本節要點提示

- 副詞最重要的問題，是在句子中的「位置」安排。

問題 1　副詞和形容詞有什麼區別？

➡語法功能

形容詞：修飾名詞、充當補語。

副詞：修飾名詞之外的其他成分（包括謂語動詞、形容詞、副詞、介詞短語、非謂語動詞結構和整個句子）。

＊少數特別的情況下，副詞也可以修飾動名詞或者名詞類結構。比如：

Exercises, especially jogging, are good for your health.

➡在句子中的位置

單個形容詞：只能出現在句子中定語和補語兩個固定位置。

副詞：位置非常靈活，但也不是完全隨意的。位置變動，修飾對象改變，句子意思可能不一樣，分三種情況：強調語氣類副詞、方法狀態類副詞、修飾句子類副詞。

問題2　強調語氣類副詞有哪些類別？

➡強調語氣類的副詞可以再細分為三種：範圍副詞、語氣副詞、程度副詞。

＊可以修飾：名詞、動詞、形容詞、副詞。

＊在句子中位置一般固定：必須緊貼修飾對象，中間不能有標點符號或其他詞。

（1）範圍副詞：only, merely, also, especially, particularly, even 等，功能在於明確討論範圍。位置不一樣，句子含義不一樣。

She goes shopping with Lily today.

only 在主語前：Only she goes shopping with Lily today.

only 在謂語前：She only goes shopping with Lily today.

only 在對象狀語前：She goes shopping only with Lily today.

only 在時間狀語前：She goes shopping with Lily only today.

(2)語氣副詞：刪除後，句子意思不變，只是有所弱化。

Thank you ~~very much~~!

He is ~~totally~~ crazy.

I ~~really~~ need some rest.

(3)程度副詞：刪除後，句子意思可能會改變。

* 表示「幾乎不」的否定副詞，對句子意思影響更大。

The job is almost finished. ≠ The job is finished.

I can hardly see it. 和 I can see it. 意思相反。

* 英語中常見的否定程度副詞有：

hardly; barely; rarely; scarcely; seldom

問題 3　方法狀態類副詞有什麼特點？

➡功能：專門修飾動詞。

➡典型的構詞：在形容詞詞尾加上 -ly。

➡位置特點：盡可能接近動詞，常在動詞後；如果動詞後面有賓語和補語，位置要向後挪；如果賓語和補語太長，副詞挪到動詞前面。

＊主謂結構：

They laugh loudly.

They laugh loudly in public places.

＊主謂賓結構：

The girl talks something excitedly with herfriends.

＊主補語結構：

He keeps quiet resolutely.

He keeps resolutely quiet.

＊雙賓語結構：

She gives me a book.

She gives reluctantly me a book.（X）

She reluctantly gives me a book.（√）

She gives me a book reluctantly.（√）

＊賓補結構：

The public elected him president unanimously.

I happily pronounce you husband and wife.

問題 4　修飾句子類副詞有什麼特點？

➡位置不固定：句子開頭結尾，或主語、謂語動詞之間；要用逗號和句子主體部分隔開。

➡連接副詞 conjunct: 功能類似於連詞，展現兩句話間的邏輯關係：

besides; furthermore=and

however; nevertheless=but

＊不同在於：副詞要用逗號與句子主體隔開。

Something happened with the producing, <u>therefore</u>, the movie is not finished in time.

In these days, <u>however</u>, people place more value on looks.

＊分離副詞 disjunct: 功能類似於「……地說」這類意思的從句簡化而成，在句子前、後都可以，但需要用逗號隔開，才是修飾整個主句的。

Generally speaking,=Generally,　一般地說

Honestly speaking,=Honestly,　老實說

Scientifically speaking,=Scientifically,　從科學角度說

077

上篇：基礎句型─掌握簡單句

＊如果沒有逗號，這類副詞就可能只是修飾句子中某個成分，而不是整個句子：

I answered his question honestly.

What is your name, honestly?

本節內容概要

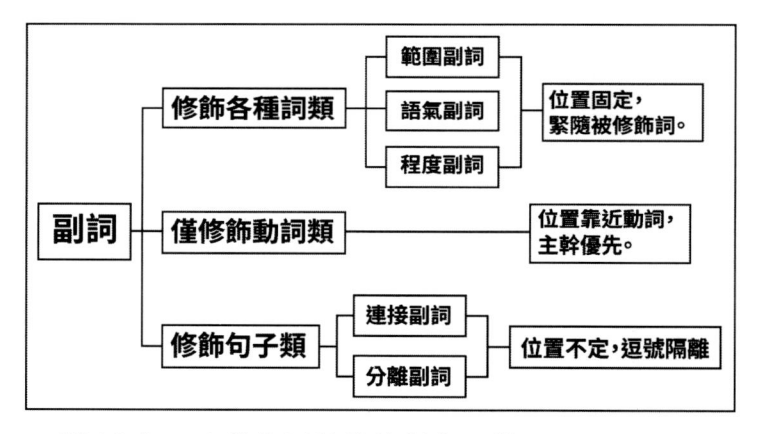

```
                    ┌─ 範圍副詞 ─┐
         修飾各種詞類 ─┼─ 語氣副詞 ─┼─ 位置固定，緊隨被修飾詞。
                    └─ 程度副詞 ─┘

副詞 ─── 僅修飾動詞類 ──────── 位置靠近動詞，主幹優先。

                    ┌─ 連接副詞 ─┐
         修飾句子類 ──┤           ├─ 位置不定，逗號隔離
                    └─ 分離副詞 ─┘
```

副詞在句子中的位置隨修飾對象而變：

1. 可以修飾任何詞類的副詞，必須在緊隨被修飾詞的固定位置。
2. 專門修飾動詞的副詞，盡量靠近動詞，可前可後。
3. 修飾整個句子的副詞，位置靈活，但要用逗號隔開。

十二　介詞

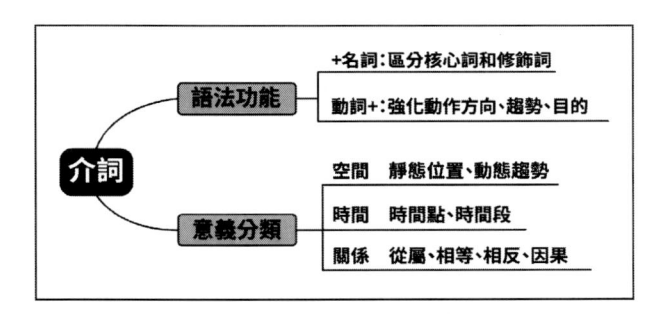

十二　介詞

```
                    ┌─ +名詞：區分核心詞和修飾詞
         ┌─ 語法功能 ┤
         │          └─ 動詞+：強化動作方向、趨勢、目的
   介詞 ─┤
         │          ┌─ 空間   靜態位置、動態趨勢
         └─ 意義分類 ┼─ 時間   時間點、時間段
                    └─ 關係   從屬、相等、相反、因果
```

本節要點提示

- 清楚辨析介詞之間的含義差別，對於準確運用介詞，至關重要。

問題1　介詞的語法功能是什麼？

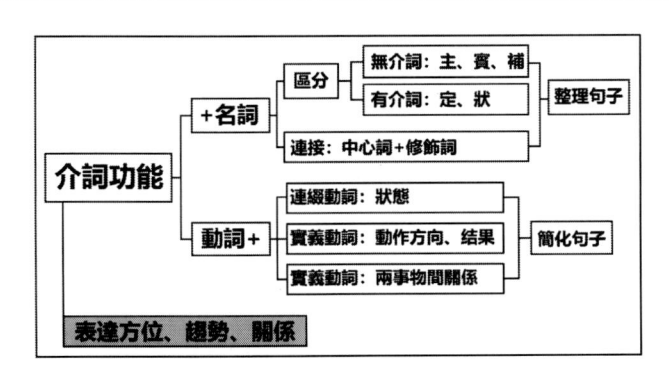

```
                        ┌─ 無介詞：主、賓、補
              ┌─ 區分  ─┤                      ─ 整理句子
         +名詞┤         └─ 有介詞：定、狀
              │
              └─ 連接：中心詞+修飾詞
  介詞功能 ─┤
              ┌─ 連綴動詞：狀態
              │
         動詞+┼─ 實義動詞：動作方向、結果  ─ 簡化句子
              │
              └─ 實義動詞：兩事物間關係

   表達方位、趨勢、關係
```

➡ 與名詞搭配

名詞：作主幹成分主語、賓語、補語

介詞後的名詞：作修飾成分定語、狀語。

「介詞＋名詞」作後置定語，翻譯口訣：A of B=B 的 A，其中的 of 可以換成其他介詞。

＊作用 1：釐清名詞主次地位：介詞前是中心詞，介詞後是修飾詞。

介詞是一種「語法象徵」詞，是一個名詞的語法身分標籤。一般當一個名詞前有介詞時，說明其身分為修飾詞而非核心詞。而且介詞一般短小，與標點符號一樣容易從句子中識別出來。

➡ 與動詞搭配

be 動詞後的介詞或介詞＋名詞用作補語；

高頻動詞後的介詞表示方向和結果。

＊作用 2：簡化句子陳述。

介詞是位置、方向、關係終極抽象概括的結果，有時在不需要精準的狀況下，可以取代形容詞、副詞和動詞來簡化句子陳述。

問題 2　介詞運用上有什麼難點？

➡介詞含義不具體；

➡介詞＋抽象名詞，介詞＋具體名詞，表示方位之外的用法；

➡介詞＋作為次要修飾成分的名詞，能整理句子結構；

➡介詞代替動詞表示動態趨勢、關係，能簡化句子。

問題 3　介詞與方位名詞有什麼關係？

➡表示方位的名詞，可以和介詞組成短語來描述位置。

頂部　top、底部　bottom ←→ on the top of; at the bottom of

左邊　left、右邊　right ←→ on the left of; on the right of

前面　front、後面　back ←→ in front of; in/on/at the back of

中心　center、裡面　inside、外面　out/outside ←→ in the center of/out of

問題 4　50 個常用介詞應該如何分類整理？

➡可以依據表達功能，將介詞分為空間、時間和關係三類。

上篇：基礎句型—掌握簡單句

(1)空間：分為「靜態位置」和「動態趨勢」兩種。

＊靜態位置 —— 上下　at: 在一個點上；on: 支撐；over: 超越，覆蓋；above: 達標，超過；under: 被覆蓋下的；below: 低於，沒達到；beneath: 貼近下面

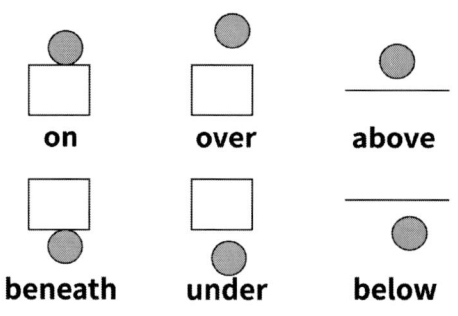

on　　**over**　　**above**

beneath　　**under**　　**below**

靜態位置 —— 前後　before: 發生在……之前的，位置靠前的；behind: 位置靠後的；after: 發生在……之後的

靜態位置 —— 內外　in: 內；around: 周圍；out: 外

靜態位置 —— 遠近　by: 緊貼一旁；beside: 緊貼旁邊；near: 離得不遠；about: 離得不遠，關於；beyond: 離得很遠，碰不到

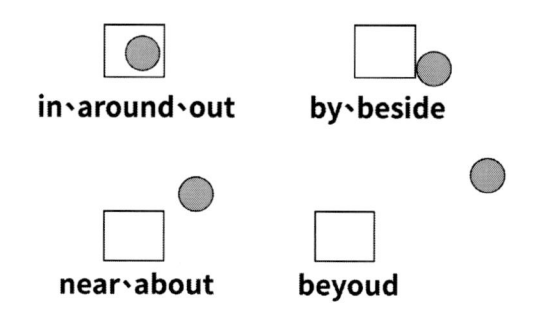

in、around、out　　**by、beside**

near、about　　**beyoud**

十二 介詞

靜態位置──之間　between+（可數名詞）：兩者間；among+（可數名詞）：三者及以上間；amid+（不可數名詞）：其間

動態趨勢──離開　from: 離開（由彼及此）；away: 離開（由此及彼）；off: 從連接到分離（切換）；down: 從上往下（過程）；up: 從下往上（過程）

動態趨勢──經過　through: 從一頭到另一頭；across: 從一側到另一側；over: 從一點到另一點；pass: 經過一個點

動態趨勢──到達　to/toward/into/onto: 到……

(2)時間：分為接時間點和接時間段兩種情況。

* 區分銜接時間的　at、on、in

at: 時間點（幾點鐘、正午、周末）

on: 在某一天（星期一、幾月幾號）

in: 在一段時間內（三天、一週、一個月、一年、一個世紀）

* 接「時間點」的介詞

*since/from/after: 從……起（開始的時間）；until/by/to/before: 到……止（結束的時間）；from...to...: 從……到……

* 接「時間段」的介詞

*during: 在一段時間內；over: 經過的一段時間；for: 持續了一段時間；as: 和……同時的一段時間

(3)關係：又分為從屬關係和同等關係兩種。

*「從屬關係」of:……的（從小到大：後接主體、整體）；with: 有……的，用……的（從大到小：後接附屬、成分）；within: 在……範圍內有；without: 在……範圍內沒有；by: 用……工具、方法，透過……途徑（從小到大）　由……生產。

make from: 產品與原材料關係不直接。

make of: 產品與原材料關係直接。

死於。

die from: 死於外界原因（間接的）

die of: 死於自身的原因（直接的）

*「同等關係」besides:=and，在……之外，加一個；as: 作為……（同一個人、事、物）；like: 像……（兩個人、事、物）

十二 介詞

本節內容概要

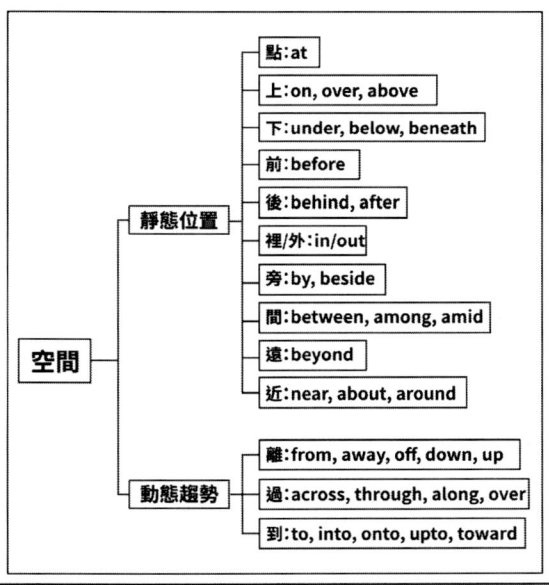

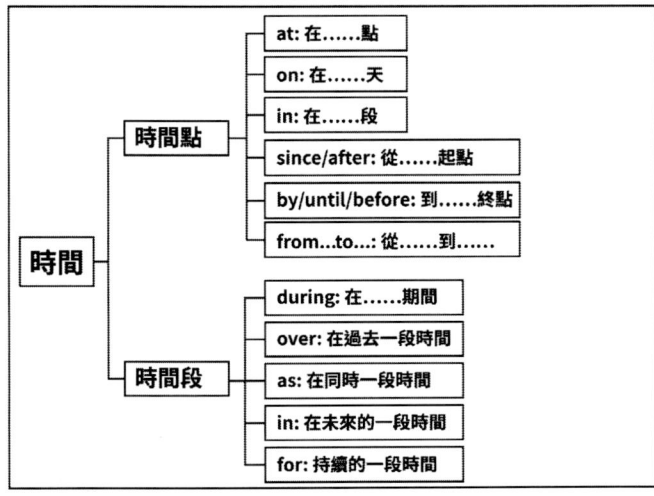

- 空間
  - 靜態位置
    - 點：at
    - 上：on, over, above
    - 下：under, below, beneath
    - 前：before
    - 後：behind, after
    - 裡/外：in/out
    - 旁：by, beside
    - 間：between, among, amid
    - 遠：beyond
    - 近：near, about, around
  - 動態趨勢
    - 離：from, away, off, down, up
    - 過：across, through, along, over
    - 到：to, into, onto, upto, toward

- 時間
  - 時間點
    - at: 在……點
    - on: 在……天
    - in: 在……段
    - since/after: 從……起點
    - by/until/before: 到……終點
    - from...to...: 從……到……
  - 時間段
    - during: 在……期間
    - over: 在過去一段時間
    - as: 在同時一段時間
    - in: 在未來的一段時間
    - for: 持續的一段時間

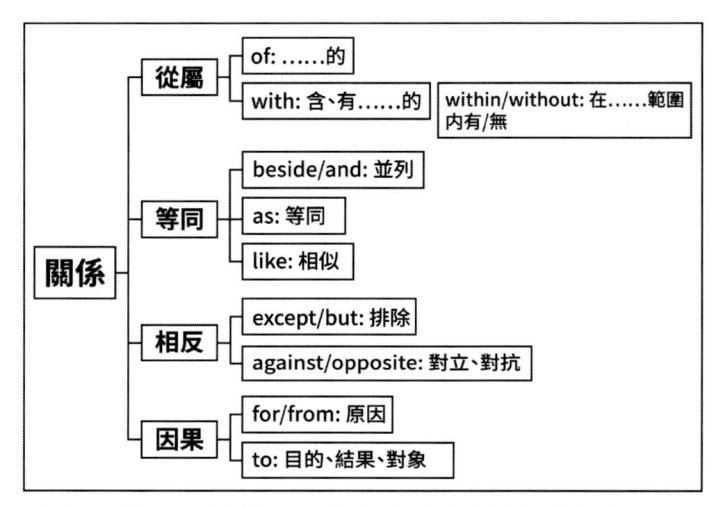

```
關係 ─┬─ 從屬 ─┬─ of: ……的
      │       ├─ with: 含、有……的
      │       └─ within/without: 在……範圍內有/無
      ├─ 等同 ─┬─ beside/and: 並列
      │       ├─ as: 等同
      │       └─ like: 相似
      ├─ 相反 ─┬─ except/but: 排除
      │       └─ against/opposite: 對立、對抗
      └─ 因果 ─┬─ for/from: 原因
              └─ to: 目的、結果、對象
```

1. 介詞是位置、趨勢、關係抽象成語法符號的結果，可以理順並簡化句子。
2. 介詞總數不多，但使用頻率極高。
3. 介詞用不好，一是因為沒有準確掌握其含義，二是因為不習慣。

上篇總結：句子中有哪些語法要素？

十二　介詞

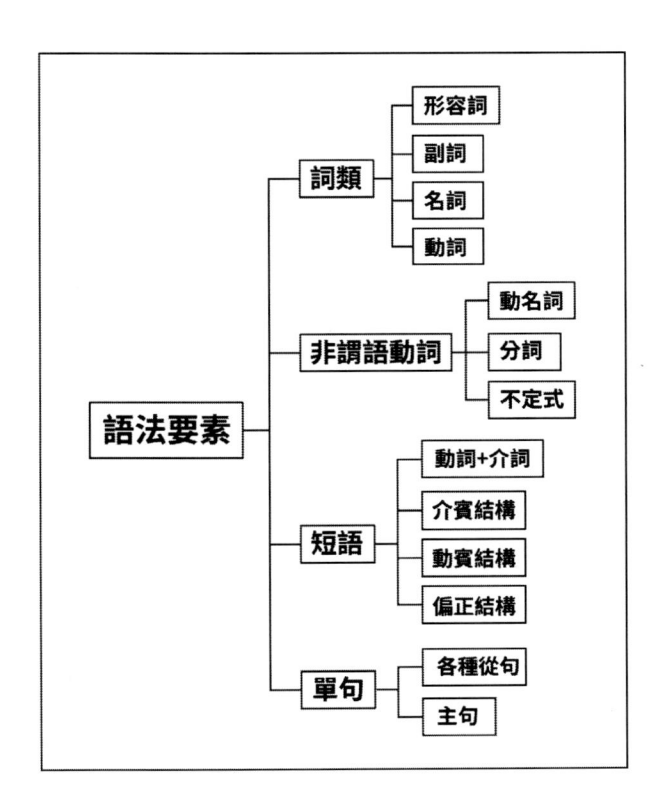

```
語法要素 ─┬─ 詞類 ─┬─ 形容詞
         │        ├─ 副詞
         │        ├─ 名詞
         │        └─ 動詞
         │
         ├─ 非謂語動詞 ─┬─ 動名詞
         │              ├─ 分詞
         │              └─ 不定式
         │
         ├─ 短語 ─┬─ 動詞+介詞
         │       ├─ 介賓結構
         │       ├─ 動賓結構
         │       └─ 偏正結構
         │
         └─ 單句 ─┬─ 各種從句
                 └─ 主句
```

上篇：基礎句型—掌握簡單句

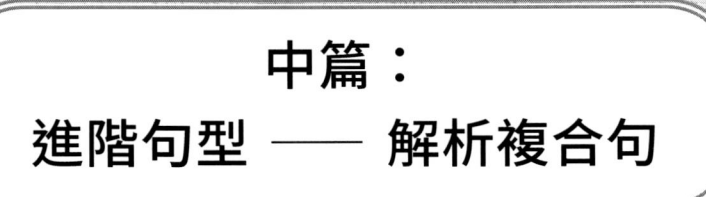

中篇：
進階句型 —— 解析複合句

中篇：進階句型—解析複合句

一 名詞從句

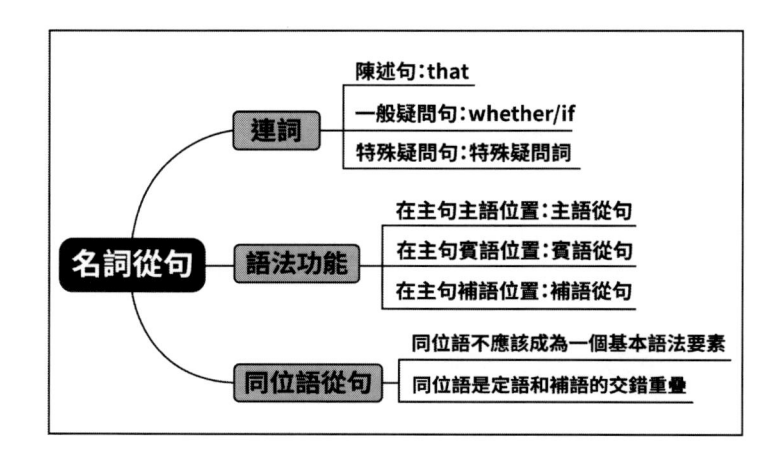

```
                    ┌─ 陳述句：that
          ┌─ 連詞 ──┼─ 一般疑問句：whether/if
          │         └─ 特殊疑問句：特殊疑問詞
          │
          │         ┌─ 在主句主語位置：主語從句
名詞從句 ─┼─ 語法功能┼─ 在主句賓語位置：賓語從句
          │         └─ 在主句補語位置：補語從句
          │
          │           ┌─ 同位語不應該成為一個基本語法要素
          └─ 同位語從句┤
                      └─ 同位語是定語和補語的交錯重疊
```

本節要點提示

- 根據名詞從句原本是陳述、一般疑問還是特殊疑問句來選擇連接詞。
- 名詞從句可以用作複句的主、賓、補等句子成分。這些都是名詞可以充當的句子成分。
- 同位語從句不是一種基本語法要素，而是一種「臨時解決方案」。

一　名詞從句

問題1　如何區分單句、複句與合句？

➡單句：只有一個（套）謂語動詞；

合句：多個（套）謂語動詞；連詞用 and、but、or；各個單句間是平行對等關係；單句間有逗號隔開。

複句：多個（套）謂語動詞；從句用專屬的連詞引導；從句是主句的一個句子成分；有些類型的從句與主句間有逗號，有些沒有。

問題2　名詞從句連詞有哪些？

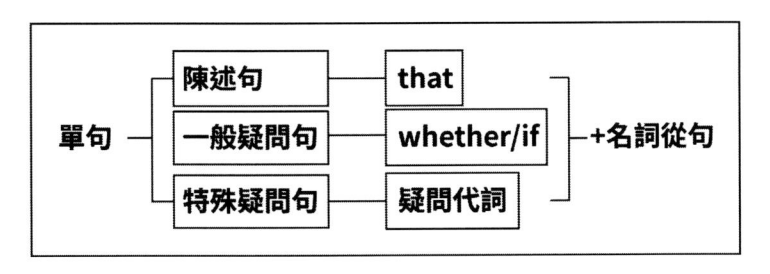

```
        ┌─ 陳述句 ───── that    ┐
單句 ───┼─ 一般疑問句 ─ whether/if ├─+名詞從句
        └─ 特殊疑問句 ─ 疑問代詞  ┘
```

➡原本為陳述句的單句，成為複句中的名詞從句時，連詞用：that，表示「那件事情」。

主句：I know something.

從句：Your book is interesting.

複句：I know that your book is interesting.

091

*that 是「額外添加」的，省略之後不影響句子切分，所以可以省略。

I think ~~that~~ I know it.=I think I know it.

➡原本為一般疑問句的單句，成為複句中的名詞從句時，連詞用：whether 或 if，表示「那個問題」。

主句：The question is hard to say.

從句：Is he telling the truth?

複句：Whether <u>he is telling the truth</u> is hard to say.

* 連詞是從句的成分，刪除之後句子的疑問會轉為陳述，不能省略。

*if 與 whether 大多可互換，但從句在句首或介詞之後時，只用 whether。

主句：The future of our company depends on the question.

從句：Will Jack or Lee be the CEO?

複句：The future of our company depends on whether <u>Jack or Lee will be the CEO</u>.

➡原本為一般疑問句的單句，成為複句中的名詞從句時，連詞用：what, who, when, where 等，表示「那個問題」。

主句：I know the question.

從句：Who are you?

一　名詞從句

複句：I know who you are.

* 連詞是從句的成分，不能省略。

問題 3　根據在句子中的位置，名詞從句有哪些語法功能？

➡名詞從句在主句主語位置：主語從句。

主句：Something changed his decision.

從句：Jack didn't show up.

複句：That Jack didn't show up changed his decision.

* 從句長，主句短，主語位置可用形式主語 it 占位，主語從句後置。

主句：Something is strange.

從句：Jack doesn't show up on time.

複句：It is strange that Jack doesn't show up on time.

➡名詞從句在主句賓語位置：賓語從句。

主句：The girl said something.

從句：Jack didn't show up.

複句：The girl said that Jack didn't show up.

* 賓語從句比主句重要，是觀點部分；主句可看作「賓語從句外殼」。

中篇：進階句型—解析複合句

The girl said Jack didn't show up.

=「Jack didn't show up,」said the girl.

＊連詞 that：在主語從句中不能省略；在賓語從句中可以省略。

That Jack didn't show up changed his decision.（X）

The girl said that Jack didn't show up.（√）

＊從句在主句補語位置：補語從句。

The current situation is (that) we are better than them.

問題 4　什麼是「同位語從句」？

同位語與語法系統中其他概念交錯重疊，不是一個獨立的基本要素

與定語重疊：The story that he killed a man might be true.

與補語重疊：I am afraid that I can't help you.

本節內容概要

1. 名詞從句的三種主要連接詞：that，表示「那件事情」；whether/if，表示「是否」；疑問詞 who/what/when/where 等，表示「那個問題」。

一　名詞從句

2. 名詞從句的位置，就是一個句子中名詞類成分的位置，包括謂語動詞之前的主語、及物動詞之後的賓語以及繫動詞之後的補語。

中篇：進階句型—解析複合句

二　形容詞從句

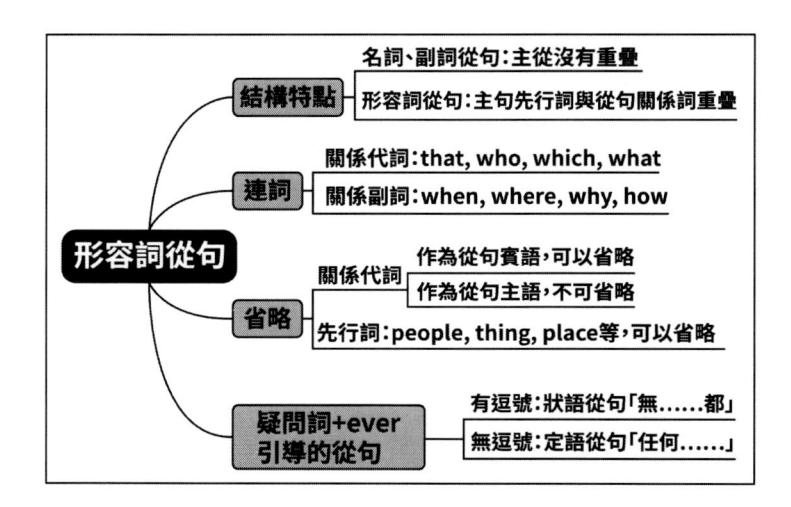

```
形容詞從句
├─ 結構特點
│    ├─ 名詞、副詞從句：主從沒有重疊
│    └─ 形容詞從句：主句先行詞與從句關係詞重疊
├─ 連詞
│    ├─ 關係代詞：that, who, which, what
│    └─ 關係副詞：when, where, why, how
├─ 省略
│    ├─ 關係代詞
│    │    ├─ 作為從句賓語，可以省略
│    │    └─ 作為從句主語，不可省略
│    └─ 先行詞：people, thing, place等，可以省略
└─ 疑問詞+ever引導的從句
     ├─ 有逗號：狀語從句「無……都」
     └─ 無逗號：定語從句「任何……」
```

本節要點提示

- 形容詞從句＝定語從句＝關係從句，是三種複合句中最難的一種。
- 關係從句的難點在於主句先行詞與從句關係詞重疊。

096

二 形容詞從句

問題1 為什麼關係從句又叫作形容詞從句和定語從句？

➡形容詞從句：從句語法功能相當於形容詞的詞類；

➡定語從句：在主句中充當定語的句子成分；

➡關係從句：從句的結構特點。

問題2 關係從句有什麼結構特點？

＊名詞／副詞從句：從句和主句是分開的兩部分，透過連詞組合。

＊關係從句：從句的連詞「關係詞」與主句的「先行詞」重疊。

主句：I meet a nice girl.

從句：The girl is in the same college with me.

複句：I meet a nice girl who is in the same college with me.

➡關係詞 who 三重功能：連接主從句；與先行詞重疊關連；充當從句句子成分。

問題3 關係從句的連接詞有哪些？

＊關係代詞：that/who/whom/which/what 在從句中用作主、賓、補語；whose 用作從句中某個名詞類結構的限定詞。

中篇：進階句型—解析複合句

* 關係副詞：when/where/why/how 在從句中用作狀語。

* 關係詞對應的先行詞內容：that ←→指示功能

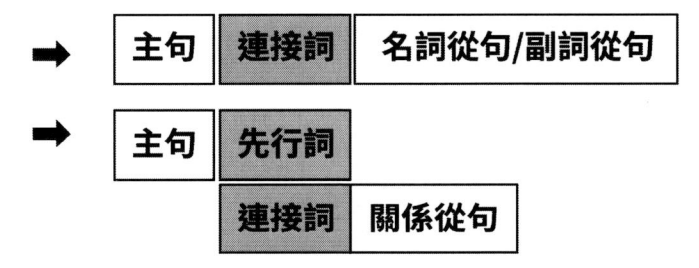

➡ | 主句 | 連接詞 | 名詞從句/副詞從句 |

➡ | 主句 | 先行詞 |
      | 連接詞 | 關係從句 |

who/whom ←→先行詞是人

which ←→先行詞是事物

whose ←→先行詞是物主

when ←→先行詞是時間

where ←→先行詞是地點

why ←→先行詞是原因

how ←→先行詞是狀態和方式

問題4　關係代詞在什麼情況下可以省略？

➡省略之後不影響主句和從句的切分時，關係代詞就可以省略。

* 關係代詞是從句的賓語，可以省略：

I meet a nice girl ~~who~~ my brother introduces to me.（√）

二　形容詞從句

＊關係代詞是從句主語，不可省略：

The girl ~~who~~ was here just now is very nice.

The girl was here just now is very nice.（X）

問題 5　什麼條件下，可以用 that 作關係代詞？

➡關係從句有指示功能時才使用 that 作關係代詞，翻譯成「那個……的某某人／事物」。

Psychology is a science that researches people's mind consciously.

➡先行詞有形容詞最高級形式或 only 等修飾的時候：

Money is the only thing that interests him.

He is the best man that I have ever met.

➡關係從句沒有指示功能，只是補充說明的性質，就不能用 that，最典型的是「非限定性定語從句」，用逗號和主句隔開。

Professor Lee, who is very famous in this field, will give us a speech this afternoon.

Shakespeare, who was born in 1564, was the most famous English writer.

＊非限定性定語從句：逗號和關係詞不能省略，不以 that 作關係詞。

099

問題6 關係代詞前的先行詞，
　　　　在什麼情況下可以省略？

➡先行詞是 people 和 thing 這類空洞的類別詞，而關係代詞 who 本身就有人的意義，what 本身就有事物的意義，這時候，先行詞可省略。

You can take any bag you like.（先行詞含義具體，不可省略）

You can take what you like.（anything which=what）

They shoot the girl who moves.（先行詞含義具體，不可省略）

They shoot whoever moves.（anybody who=who）

＊上述省略 thing 和 people 的關係從句形式上類似於賓語從句，但本質上只是省略先行詞的關係從句。

問題7 關係副詞引導的關係從句與狀語從句
　　　　有何區別？

➡如果先行詞是一種時間、地點、原因、方式或狀態，從句要用對應的關係副詞 when/where/why/how。

主句：We get the money at a time.

從句：We need the money at the time.

複句：We get the money (at a time) when we need it.

➡ when/where/why/how 詞形上較接近關係詞 which/who/what；與狀語從句連接詞 because/if/though 等引導的狀語從句，語法功能完全不同。

問題 8　關係副詞前的先行詞，在什麼情況下可以省略？

➡ 先行詞表示時間、地點時，關係詞用副詞 when、where；

＊先行詞是主句的主幹成分（主語、賓語）時，不能省略：

主句：I need a place.

從句：I can finish my work quietly at the place.

複句：I need a place where I can finish my work quietly.

＊先行詞是主句的修飾成分（時間、地點狀語）時，可以省略：

主句：I finished my work at a place.

從句：I can be quiet at the place.

複句：I finished my work (at a place) where I can be quiet.

總之：

中篇：進階句型—解析複合句

　　*who 本身有「人」的意思，主句先行詞 people/person 可被省略。

　　what 本身有「事物」的意思，所以主句先行詞 thing 可被省略。

　　when 本身有「在……時候」的意思，主句先行詞 at a time 可被省略。

　　where 本身有「在……地方」的意思，主句先行詞 at aplace 可被省略。

問題 9 「疑問詞＋後綴 -ever」構成的連接詞引導的從句有什麼特點？

　　➡可能是關係從句或者狀語從句，主要看主、從句之間有沒有逗號。

　　* 有逗號：＝ no matter+ 疑問詞（讓步狀語從句），「無論……都……」

Whenever I visit her, she appears so happy.

= No matter when I visit her, she appears so happy.

Whatever he may say, it won't change my mind.

= No matter what he may say, it won't change my mind.

二 形容詞從句

＊無逗號：＝ any+ 疑問詞（關係從句），「任何……」

I will visit her whenever she is happy.

= I will visit her at anytime when she is happy.

He will do whatever pleases her.

= He will do anything that pleases her.

本節內容概要

1. 複句中的三種從句：名詞從句、副詞從句和形容詞從句，區別關鍵在於連接詞。連接詞是從句的語法身分標示。
2. 副詞從句的連接詞自成體系，有具體的邏輯含義，分類比較細膩。
3. 名詞從句和關係從句的連接詞是含義相對寬泛的指示代詞 that 和疑問代詞 who/whom/what/which/whose/when/where/why/whether/how。
4. 關係從句的連接詞，最重要的特點是所指的內容與主句中的先行詞重疊。

中篇：進階句型—解析複合句

三 副詞從句

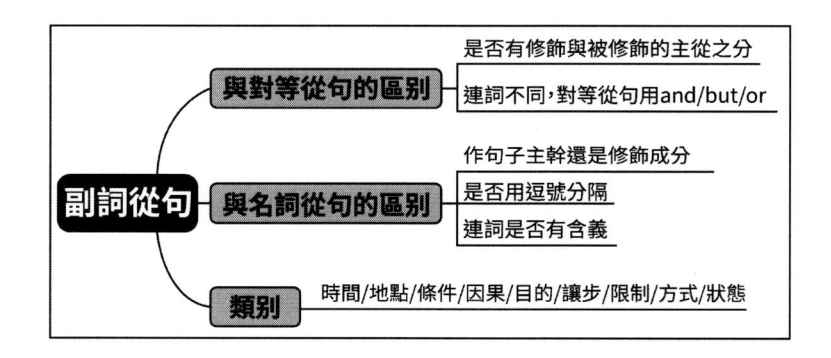

```
                          ┌── 是否有修飾與被修飾的主從之分
         ┌─ 與對等從句的區別 ─┤
         │                 └── 連詞不同，對等從句用and/but/or
         │
         │                 ┌── 作句子主幹還是修飾成分
副詞從句 ─┼─ 與名詞從句的區別 ─┼── 是否用逗號分隔
         │                 └── 連詞是否有含義
         │
         └─ 類別 ── 時間/地點/條件/因果/目的/讓步/限制/方式/狀態
```

本節要點提示

- 狀語從句也叫副詞從句，因為副詞的語法功能是作狀語。
- 狀語從句與對等從句根本區別在於，兩個從句間的地位是否平等。
- 狀語從句學習的重點在於連接詞表示的具體邏輯關係。
- when、while、why、where 等引導的狀語從句可算作定語從句。

三　副詞從句

問題1　狀語從句與對等從句有什麼區別？

＊狀語從句（副詞從句）是複句的三種從句（名詞從句、形容詞從句、副詞從句）中最容易分析的，因為從句和主句間一般有逗號，且連接詞有相對具體的含義，不能刪。

狀語從句和對等從句的相同點：都用逗號隔開，連接詞不能刪。

<u>Because</u> she wants to master English, she studies hard.

She wants to master English<u>, and</u> she studies hard.

➡狀語從句和對等從句的不同點：

＊狀語從句屬於複句，與主句是修飾與被修飾的關係，地位不對等，對等從句屬於合句，各單句間地位平等。

＊對等從句的連接詞只能用 and/but/or；狀語從句的連詞，根據邏輯關係，種類很多：

如 if（條件），although（讓步），because（因果）……

問題2　狀語從句與名詞從句有什麼區別？

She said <u>that she knew it</u>.（賓語從句）

She said that, <u>though she didn't know it</u>.（狀語從句）

➡去掉名詞從句，主句不完整；去掉狀語從句，主句依然完整。

中篇：進階句型—解析複合句

名詞從句與主句間不用逗號句隔開；狀語從句常用逗號隔開。

名詞從句的連接詞含義不具體；狀語從句的連接詞含義具體。

問題 3　狀語從句有哪些類型？

(1)時間、地點狀語從句。

連接詞有兩種：

第一種本身有時空位置意味：before/after/until

I will be home before the dinner is ready.

第二種是疑問詞：when/while/where/why

I will be home when the dinner is ready.

(2)條件狀語從句。

連接詞：if/as long as/suppose 等。

*if/as long as 是條件語氣，從句用現在時，主句情態動詞用 will：

If she calls, I will answer the phone.

*suppose 習慣上寫成動詞原形：

Suppose you were me, what would you do?

(3) 原因、結果狀語從句。

原因連詞：as/since/because/for 等；

結果連詞或副詞：so/thus/therefore/hence 等。

* 原因連詞和結果連詞不能連用，避免兩個狀語從句，而沒有主句。

<u>As the computer is broken</u>, I need to buy a new one.

The computer is broken, <u>so I need to buy a new one</u>.

* 狀語從句能不能用 that 作為連詞？

in that: 原因在於（原因狀語從句）

so that: 所以（結果狀語從句）

now that: 既然（讓步狀語從句）

in order that: 為了（目的狀語從句）

* 區別：so that/so+ 形容詞 +that（如此……以致於）有區別：

She looks <u>so sincere that</u> everybody believes her story.

She looks sincere <u>so that</u> everybody believes her story

(4) 目的狀語從句。

連詞：

➡積極目的：「為了……」so that/in order that

➡消極目的：「以免……」in case that/lest

*so that/in order that 既是結果狀語，又是目的狀語。

* 如何區分結果和目的？

結果：客觀上的，已經發生的。

She looks sincere so that everybody believes her story.

目的：主觀上的，未發生的。

I put on a red coat so that they can notice me.

*in case that 和 lest 是目的而非因果。

I put on a red coat lest they (should) miss me.

I should take more money, in case that I should need it.

* 只要是事情沒有真實發生，就要考慮用假設語氣，如果沒有用情態動詞，說明說話人主觀上認為可能性很大。

(5)讓步狀語從句。

連詞：though/although/while「儘管……」；no matter+ 疑問詞、疑問詞 +ever 後綴等表示「無論……都」。

*though 和 although 的區別在於：

although 語氣更強，一般位於句首，而 though 用於句首句中都可以；although 一般接真實發生的事情，不用於假設語氣，而 though 則可以用於假設語氣。

even 可以搭配 though，而不能搭配 although。

Though all the world were against me, I would insist my opinion.

Although everybody tells him not to, he still insists on going there.

疑問詞＋ever，或 no matter...＋疑問詞，引導的讓步狀語從句：

Whoever calls, I will not answer.（無論誰……都不）

= No matter who calls, I will not answer.

Wherever he goes, I will catch him.（無論哪……都要）

= No matter where he goes, I will catch him.

(6)限制狀語從句。

連詞：as far as「就……而言」；in the sense that「從某種意義來說」（＝介詞短語 as to...「至於說……」）。

As far as money is concerned, you needn't worry.

= As to the money, you needn't worry.

(7)方式、狀態狀語從句。

連詞：as/as if「按照……」（＝介詞短語 according to;by/in the way...「根據……」）。

He writes as if he is left-handed.（按左撇子的方式：實際是）

= He writes by the way of his left hand.

中篇：進階句型─解析複合句

*as if 從句也可以用假設語氣，表示「好像……一樣」而其實不是。區別在於謂語動詞的時態是否用過去式。

He writes as if he was left-handed.（像左撇子的方式：實際不是）

本節內容概要

1. 狀語從句也叫副詞從句，是修飾性從句，與主句的地位不對等。
2. 狀語從句的連接詞有區分含義的功能，大致可以概括為 7 類。在條件、讓步、目的等從句中表達未真實發生的情況時，要考慮用假設語氣。

四 對等從句

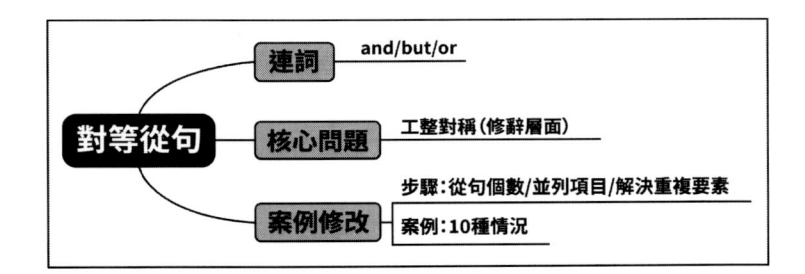

```
對等從句 ─┬─ 連詞 ──── and/but/or
          ├─ 核心問題 ── 工整對稱(修辭層面)
          └─ 案例修改 ┬─ 步驟:從句個數/並列項目/解決重複要素
                      └─ 案例:10種情況
```

本節要點提示

- and、but、or 既可以用作介詞連接兩個或多個詞和詞組,也可以用作連詞連接兩個或多個句子,但所連接的內容必須工整對稱。
- 對稱具體要求包括內容相關,也包括語法結構相似。

問題 1　and/but/or 連接的內容有什麼對稱要求？

*介詞 and/but/or: 連接兩個或多個詞和詞組(無謂語動詞);

* 連詞 and/but/or: 連接兩個或多個句子(有謂語動詞)。

and/but/or 兩邊的內容必須對稱:內容相關,語法結構相似。

問題 2　什麼是合句／對等從句？

包含有 and、but、or 的句子，都算作對等從句，要考慮對稱問題。

and: 並列關係；but: 轉折關係；or: 選擇關係。

處理對等從句中的各種對稱問題，需要綜合運用所有的語法概念；讓句子更簡明、工整對稱，屬於句子的修辭，修辭是語法的高級階段。

問題 3　如何檢查並修改一個句子的對稱問題？

➡第一，搞清楚有幾套謂語動詞（幾個從句）；對等連詞（and/but/or）出現在什麼位置。

第二，連詞右邊的內容向左邊的看齊；多項並列時，少的向多的看齊。

第三，連詞左右兩邊相應位置重複元素，用代詞、助動詞等替代，或刪除。

問題 4　句子中可能存在的對稱問題（含及修改案例）有哪些？

情況 1：詞類與詞類對稱

錯誤案例：Beijing, Capital city, the political and cultural center of China, and important as an economic center is suffering terribly smog.（X）

修改案例：Beijing, Capital city, the political, cultural and important economic center of China is suffering terribly smog. (√)

情況2：介賓結構與介賓結構對稱

錯誤案例：Smog is caused by industrial pollution, traffic emission, reduction of forests and climatic change. (X)

修改案例：Smog is caused by industrial pollution, traffic emission, reducing forests and climatic change. (√)

情況3：動賓結構與動賓結構對稱

錯誤案例：Many parents worry that smog may slow the growth of their children and it may eventually harm the growth of their children. (X)

修改案例：Many parents worry that smog may slow and eventually harm the growth of their children. (√)

情況4：並列各項的語法性質一致。

錯誤案例：Information technology has changed people's ways of working, communication, entertainment and has lowered prices for learning. (X)

修改案例：Information technology has changed people's ways of working, communicating and entertaining, and lowered prices for learning. (√)

113

情況 5：主句與主句對稱。

錯誤案例：Numerous students have been inspired by Mr. Lee, the most experienced teacher in our school, and who the most popular teacher is in our school.（X）

修改案例：Mr. Lee has been the most experienced and popular teacher in our school, and inspired numerous students.（√）

情況 6：從句與從句對稱。

錯誤案例：These courses focus on efficiency of study, which has largely improved the grammar system and with largely simplified explanation over those old ones.（X）

修改案例：These courses focus on efficiency of study, which has largely improved the grammar system, and simplified explanation over those old ones.（√）

情況 7：謂語動詞與謂語動詞對稱；非謂語動詞與非謂語動詞對稱。

錯誤案例：My new year resolution includes reading 100 books, making as much money as I can, and keep fit.（X）

修改案例：My new year resolution includes reading 100 books, making as much money as I can, and keeping fit.（√）

四　對等從句

情況 8：動名詞與動名詞對稱；不定詞與不定詞對稱。

錯誤案例：It is possible for me to drop the old plan or starting a new plan at the same time.（X）

修改案例：It is possible for me to drop the old plan or start a new one at the same time.（√）

情況 9：倒裝問題。

錯誤案例：Not only does China have the world's largest population, but also the largest market.（X）

修改案例：Not only does China have the world's largest population, but also has the largest market.（√）

情況 10：分號問題。

分號只能連接兩個從句，不能連接兩個詞或詞組。

錯誤案例：Playing video games for a very long time can be harmful to your eyesight; reading paper books, which benefits our study, actually far less harmful to your eyesight.（X）

修改案例：Playing video games for a very long time can be harmful to your eyesight; reading paper books, which benefits our study, can actually be far less harmful.（√）

中篇：進階句型—解析複合句

本節內容概要

句子的對稱，是一種修辭能力要求，是對各項語法系統基本要素及其屬性的綜合、靈活運用。

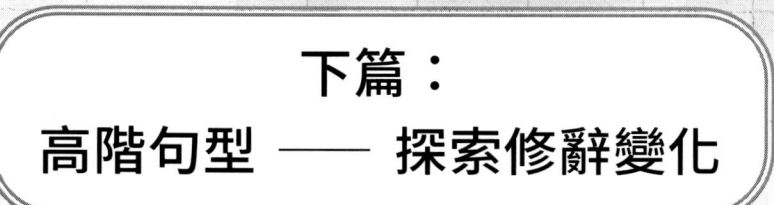

下篇：
高階句型 —— 探索修辭變化

下篇：高階句型—探索修辭變化

一　複句簡化

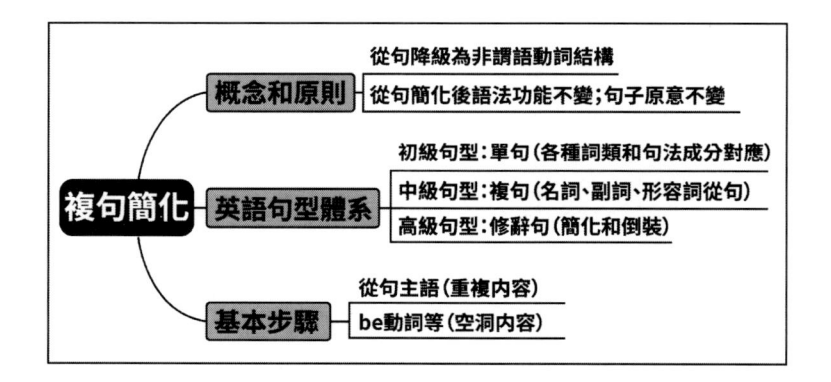

```
                    ┌─ 從句降級為非謂語動詞結構
         ┌─ 概念和原則 ─┤
         │           └─ 從句簡化後語法功能不變；句子原意不變
         │
         │           ┌─ 初級句型：單句(各種詞類和句法成分對應)
複句簡化 ─┼─ 英語句型體系 ─┼─ 中級句型：複句(名詞、副詞、形容詞從句)
         │           └─ 高級句型：修辭句(簡化和倒裝)
         │
         │         ┌─ 從句主語(重複內容)
         └─ 基本步驟 ─┤
                   └─ be動詞等(空洞內容)
```

本節要點提示

- 複句簡化，就是把從句轉變為非謂語動詞結構，使複句轉為單句。
- 從句在句子中的語法功能，非謂語動詞都可以實現。
- 複句簡化，原則是不能改變句子原本的意思。

一　複句簡化

問題1　本書上、中、下篇對應初、中、高級句型各指什麼？

初級句型：詞＋詞＝單句；語法成分是詞類。

中級句型：句＋句＝複／合句；語法成分是詞類和單句。

高級句型：複、合句 —— 重複空洞內容；包括簡化句和倒裝句。

＊單句只有5種基本句型，表達力單薄，文章中需要一些複句、合句，表達較為複雜的意思，豐富句式的變化。

＊複句、合句在內容上出現重複、空洞的成分，進行精簡能讓句子更加簡明。高級句型是對於語法知識的綜合運用，屬於語法的高階：修辭。

問題2　什麼是複句簡化？需要遵循什麼原則？

複句簡化：從句降級為語法功能相同的非謂語動詞結構。

原則：句子原本的意思不變。

問題3　複句簡化的基本步驟是什麼？

➜合句簡化：刪除，或以代詞、助動詞來替換重複元素。

➜複句簡化：

(1)省略從句連詞、主語；

(2)從句謂語動詞轉化成非謂語；名詞從句簡化成動名詞或不定詞；形容詞從句和副詞從句簡化成分詞。

(3)最終把多層結構變為單層結構。

問題 4　從句主語要如何簡化？

➡從句主語與主句中內容重複，或者從句主語是 people/thing/one/everybody/everything 等內容空洞的詞，省略之後，句子的意思不變，表達更精簡。

It is not unusual that people will risk their safety for huge profit.

簡化為：It is not unusual to risk safety for huge profit.

Professor Lee, who is a famous expert in this field, will give us a speech this afternoon.

簡化為：Professor Lee, a famous expert in this field, will give us a speech this afternoon.

＊同位語不是基本語法要素，是非限定性定語從句簡化的結果。

問題 5　從句 be 動詞要如何簡化？

根據補語不同，分三種情況：

一　複句簡化

(1)分詞作補語：刪除繫動詞（be 動詞）。

The person who is giving a speech now is Professor Lee.

簡化為：The person giving a speech now is Professor Lee.

The speech that is given by professor Lee is about globalization.

簡化為：The speech given by professor Lee is about globalization.

(2)形容詞作補語，有兩種處理方式。

＊刪除繫動詞（be 動詞），把形容詞放到名詞類結構中修飾詞位置。

I enjoy drinking coffee that is hot.

簡化為：I enjoy drinking hot coffee.

＊刪除繫動詞（be 動詞），保留形容詞，用逗號與主句隔開。

Lily, who is pretty and nice, is very popular in high school.

簡化為：Lily, pretty and nice, is very popular in high school.

(3)名詞作補語：刪除繫動詞（be 動詞），補語轉化成同位語。

Professor Lee, a famous expert in this field, will give us a speech this afternoon.

下篇：高階句型—探索修辭變化

問題 6　從句的情態動詞要如何簡化？

➡ 轉化為不定詞。

I produce this course seriously so that I will get common approval.

簡化為：I produce this course seriously to get common approval.

問題 7　從句的一般動詞要如何簡化？

➡ 轉變成分詞、動名詞。

I enjoy that I talk about my new book with some friends.

簡　化　為：I enjoy talking about my new book with some friends.

本節內容概要

從句簡化相關的步驟包括：

1. 刪除連詞和從句主語。
2. 刪除繫動詞。
3. 情態動詞變不定詞符號 to。
4. 一般動詞變分詞。其中，現在分詞表主動，過去分詞表被動。

二　形容詞從句簡化

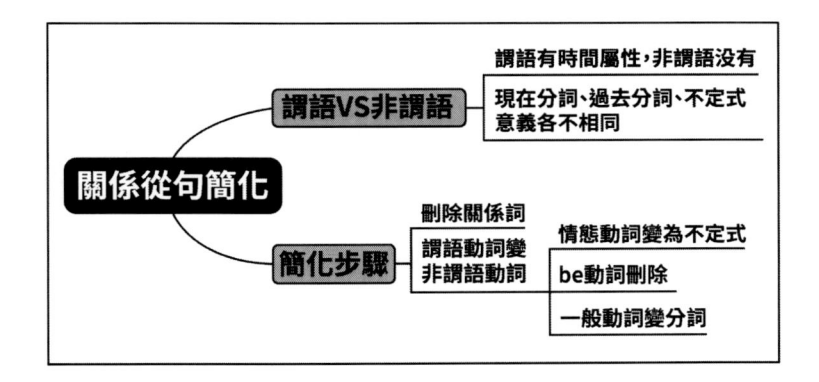

```
                               ┌─ 謂語有時間屬性，非謂語沒有
                  謂語VS非謂語 ─┤
                               └─ 現在分詞、過去分詞、不定式
關係從句簡化 ─┤                    意義各不相同
                               ┌─ 刪除關係詞        ┌─ 情態動詞變為不定式
                  簡化步驟 ─────┤  謂語動詞變 ──────┤  be動詞刪除
                               └─ 非謂語動詞        └─ 一般動詞變分詞
```

本節要點提示

- 形容詞從句又叫定語從句或關係從句。
- 關係從句簡化的兩個關鍵步驟。
- 謂語動詞與非謂語動詞各自的特點。
- 各種非謂語動詞形態可以疊加表多重含義。

下篇：高階句型—探索修辭變化

問題 1　關係從句簡化的兩個關鍵步驟是什麼？

第一，刪除關係詞；

第二，從句謂語動詞變成非謂語形式。

問題 2　謂語動詞和非謂語動詞各有什麼特性？

* 謂語動詞有時間屬性：

過去時間用過去式，現在時間用現在式，將來時間用情態動詞 will。

* 非謂語動詞沒有時間屬性，但有特定含義：

現在分詞有「進行、主動」含義；

過去分詞有「完成、被動」含義；

不定詞有「未發生、不確定」含義。

可借助 be 動詞或助動詞 have, 疊加多重形式，多重含義：

	主動	被動	完成	進行
Ving	不變	being+Ven	having+Ven	不變
Ven	無	不變	不變	無
to V	不變	to be Ven	to have Ven	to be Ving

二 形容詞從句簡化

問題 3　關係從句的關係詞要如何刪除？

➡關係代詞作從句賓語：一般只刪除關係詞，從句其他部分不變。

Is there anything ~~which~~ you want?

=Is there anything you want?

➡關係代詞是從句主語：刪除關係詞，並簡化從句謂語。

Is there anything ~~which~~ interests you?

=Is there anything interesting to you?

Is there anything ~~which~~ is interesting?

=Is there anything interesting?

Is there anyone ~~who~~ can help you?

=Is there anyone to help you?

➡關係副詞 where、when、why 引導的特殊關係從句：

一般算作副詞從句，而副詞從句引導詞不可省略；除非先行詞是表示地點的 place、somewhere，時間 time、year，原因 reason 等。

This is the place ~~where~~ we met yesterday.

I will go any time ~~when~~ you want me to.

This is the reason ~~why~~ I love you.

125

問題 4　從句中的情態動詞應如何簡化，有什麼注意事項？

➡情態動詞變為不定詞符號 to。

Bob is the one who can win the first prize this time.

=Bob is the one to win the first prize this time.

➡不定詞的三個注意事項：

(1)主被動問題。

有些動詞具有主被動雙重含義，簡化之後如何區分，先行詞是動作發出者還是承受者？

This is the right partner who should be chosen for our project.

=This is the right partner to be chosen for our project.

* 還原從句解決不定詞的主被動歧義：

He is not a man to trust.

=He is not a man who can trust people.

=He is not a man who people can trust.

* 不定詞被動式解決不定詞主被動歧義：

to+V: 主動

to+be+Ven: 被動

二　形容詞從句簡化

He is not a man to be trusted.

（2）是否帶賓語的問題。

關係從句的謂語由情態動詞＋及物動詞構成時，簡化成 to＋及物動詞後，從句中的賓語如何處理？

＊刪除關係副詞：先行詞不是邏輯賓語，從句主謂賓完整，簡化後有賓語。

It is exactly the time when we should finish our job.

=It is exactly the time for us to finish our job.

＊刪除關係代詞：先行詞是邏輯賓語，從句簡化後動詞都不帶賓語。

It is exactly the job that we should finish now.

=It is exactly the job for us to finish now.

（3）是否搭配介詞的問題。

從句的謂語動詞原本搭配了介詞的，轉變成不定詞以後，也要搭配；否則就不用。

＊從句中的介詞被提到關係詞之前的情況，從句簡化後要還原。

This is the hardest situation with which we must deal.

=This is the hardest situation for us to deal with.

下篇：高階句型—探索修辭變化

➡從句的主語如果與主句沒有重複，不能省略時：從句謂語變為不定詞，從句主語則變為介詞短語 for+ 主語。

Tomorrow is the day ~~when~~ we should finish the job.

=Tomorrow is the day for us to finish the job.

問題 5　從句中的 be 動詞應如何簡化？

➡刪除關係詞和 be 動詞後，主語補足語轉化為定語。

＊能作補語的 4 種詞類：現在分詞、過去分詞、形容詞和名詞。

（1）be 動詞 +Ving，簡化成：後置定語（單個分詞簡化後前置）。

The man ~~who is~~ talking to my mother now is my English teacher.

=The man talking to my mother now is my English teacher.

（2）be 動詞 +Ven，簡化成：後置定語（單個分詞簡化後前置）。

The boy ~~who was~~ wounded during the football game yesterday is Bob.

=The boy wounded during the football game yesterday is Bob.

二　形容詞從句簡化

*Ven 作定語也有被動的意味：

Beer ~~which is~~ chilled to 6°C is most delicious.

=Beer chilled to 6°C is most delicious.

（3）be 動詞 +adj.。

Your friend Bob, ~~who is~~ handsome and funny, is very popular with girls.

多個並列形容詞可以作為後置定語，逗號隔開的插入語形式：

=Your friend Bob, handsome and funny, is very popular with girls.

也可以作為前置定語：

=Your handsome and funny friend Bob is very popular with girls.

（4）be 動詞 +n.，簡化成：同位語。

Mr. Green, ~~who is~~ president of our school, is giving us a speech.

=Mr. Green, president of our school, is giving us a speech.

下篇：高階句型―探索修辭變化

問題 6　一般實義動詞應如何簡化？

➡刪除關係詞，謂語 V 變為非謂語 Ving 形式。

The problem ~~which~~ caused us a lot of trouble has been solved.

=The problem causing us a lot of trouble has been solved.

＊一般實義動詞不分過去、現在，簡化後一律都變成 Ving。

如果有必要強調 V 的完成屬性，則變成 having+Ven 的結構。

=The problem having caused us a lot of trouble has been solved.

本節內容概要

關係從句簡化的操作包括 4 種：

1. 刪除關係詞。
2. 刪除 be 動詞。
3. 把情態動詞變成不定詞 to。
4. 把謂語動詞變為 Ving 形式。

二　形容詞從句簡化

在「簡化後不改變原句含義」的原則下，依具體情況選擇具體操作。

＊結合流程圖，總結簡化從句的具體操作要點：

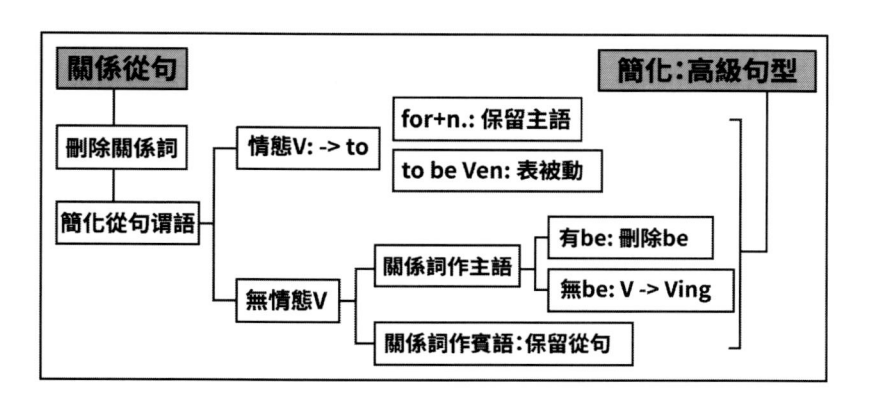

```
關係從句 ──────────────────────────────────→ 簡化:高級句型
   │
   ├─ 刪除關係詞
   │
   └─ 簡化從句謂語 ─┬─ 情態V: -> to ─┬─ for+n.: 保留主語
                   │                 └─ to be Ven: 表被動
                   │
                   └─ 無情態V ─┬─ 關係詞作主語 ─┬─ 有be: 刪除be
                              │                 └─ 無be: V -> Ving
                              │
                              └─ 關係詞作賓語: 保留從句
```

下篇：高階句型—探索修辭變化

三　名詞從句簡化

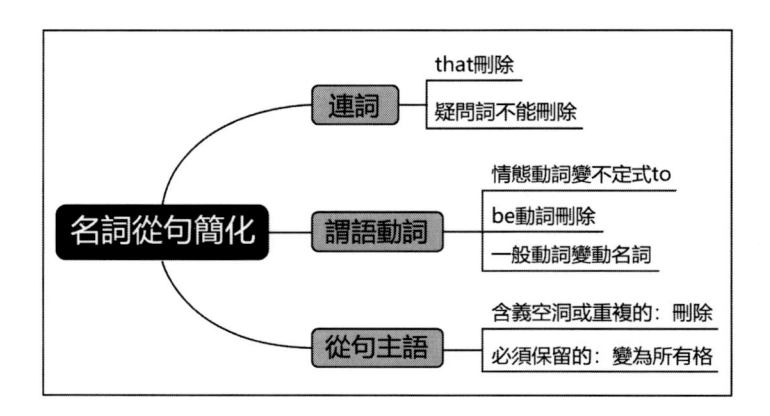

```
                          ┌── that刪除
                 ┌─ 連詞 ──┤
                 │        └── 疑問詞不能刪除
                 │
                 │           ┌── 情態動詞變不定式to
名詞從句簡化 ────┼─ 謂語動詞─┼── be動詞刪除
                 │           └── 一般動詞變動名詞
                 │
                 │           ┌── 含義空洞或重複的：刪除
                 └─ 從句主語─┤
                             └── 必須保留的：變為所有格
```

本節要點提示

- 名詞從句包括主、賓、補語從句三種，從句謂語可以簡化成動名詞和不定詞。
- 如果從句謂語是 be 動詞 +Ven，要簡化成 being+Ven。
- 疑問詞作連接詞的名詞從句，連接詞不能省略。

三　名詞從句簡化

問題 1　名詞從句的連接詞分為哪兩種情況，分別如何處理？

➡疑問詞：是從句的句子成分，在主句中沒有重複的內容，刪除後，從句可能不完整、不通順，或意思不一樣，所以不能刪除。

* 如果從句謂語中含有情態動詞，還有一定簡化空間：

I don't know <u>what I should do</u>.

簡化為：I don't know <u>what to do</u>.

* 如果從句謂語中不含情態動詞：無簡化空間，用從句表達更清晰：

I don't know <u>who she loves most</u>.

➡ that：是額外添加的語法符號，不是從句的句子成分，也沒有具體意義，刪除之後對原句意思沒有影響，所以簡化過程中要刪除。

問題 2　連接詞 that 引導的名詞從句，從句主語應如何簡化？

➡內容空洞，或與主句內容重複的從句主語，要刪除。

* 主語從句

~~That~~ I <u>write</u> this book in a quiet café is my favorite part of life.

下篇：高階句型—探索修辭變化

簡化為：Writing this book in a quiet café is my favorite part of life.

* 賓語從句

I enjoy ~~that I~~ write this book in a quiet café.

簡化為：I enjoy writing this book in a quiet café.

* 補語從句

My favorite part of life is ~~that I~~ write this book in a quiet café.

簡化為：My favorite part of life is writing this book in a quiet café.

➡ 含義具體且與主句內容不重複的從句主語，要保留：

一般不簡化，用從句表達更好。如果一定要簡化，就要改變從句主語的語法身分，主要有三種處理方式。

(1) 變為名詞所有格。

I don't like ~~that~~ my boyfriend plays video games all day.

簡化為：I don't like my boyfriend's playing video games all day.

(2) 變為主謂賓補結構。

主句謂語動詞是感官動詞或使役動詞時，賓語從句簡化為賓補結構，即：從句主語變為主句賓語，從句謂語變為主句的賓語補語。

三　名詞從句簡化

　　* 從句主語如果是代詞，要注意主賓格的切換；從句謂語變為不定詞或分詞。

I hear ~~that~~ my sister is crying.

簡化為：I hear my sister crying.

I expect ~~that~~ my boss <u>would</u> forgive my absence.

簡化為：I expect my boss <u>to</u> forgive my absence.

　　* 從說話者主觀來看，作為補語的動作是已經發生了，或是一定會發生的，就要把表示可能性的不定詞符號 to 去掉。

They make me <u>go</u> to the party.

(3) 變為介詞短語 for+n.；常搭配形式主語 it。

　　* 適用於：從句謂語有情態動詞的情況。

~~That I~~ <u>would</u> be late has been informed to the client.

簡化為：It has been informed to the client <u>for me to</u> be late.

問題 3　連接詞 that 引導的名詞從句，從句謂語應如何簡化？

分 3 種情況：

(1) 情態動詞：簡化成「不定詞」。

She expects ~~that she~~ <u>could</u> enter Harvard.

簡化為：She expects <u>to</u> enter Harvard.

下篇：高階句型—探索修辭變化

（2）be 動詞＋補語：簡化成「being+ 補語」。

＊要求：從句謂語沒有情態動詞，且 be 後的補語不是 Ving。

be+Ven 變為：being+Ven

~~That anyone~~ is mistrusted is very upsetting.

簡化為：Being mistrusted is very upsetting.

I learn ~~that you~~ are admitted to Harvard University.

簡化為：I learn your being admitted to Harvard University.

be+n./adj. 變為：being+n./adj.

~~That one~~ is a mother requires a lot of patience.

簡化為：Being a mother requires a lot of patience.

Your father always uses ~~that~~ he is busy as an excuse for absence.

簡化為：Your father always uses his being busy as an excuse for absence.

（3）V:Ving;be+Ving:Ving。

＊要求：從句謂語中不含情態動詞；從句謂語中不含 be 動詞，或者從句謂語是 be+Ving。

＊注意：簡化成非謂語動詞後，不必區分時態。

I remember ~~that I~~ washed the car yesterday.

三　名詞從句簡化

簡化為：I remember washing the car yesterday.

I enjoy ~~that I am~~ jogging with my friends.

簡化為：I enjoy jogging with my friends.

本節內容概要

1. 名詞從句謂語簡化成不定詞或動名詞。
2. 名詞從句簡化與關係從句簡化，有兩個明顯不同的方面：

    (1) 作為疑問詞的連接詞不能刪除；

    (2) be 動詞要以 ing 形式加以保留。

    * 結合流程圖，總結簡化從句的具體操作要點：

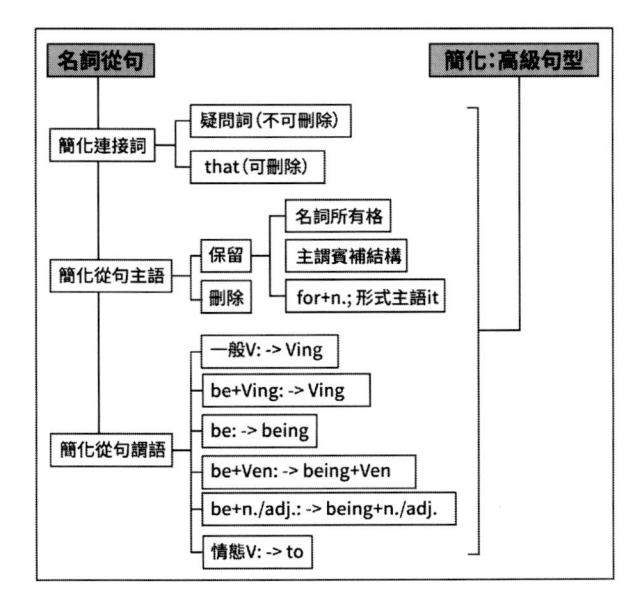

```
名詞從句                          簡化:高級句型

簡化連接詞 ─┬─ 疑問詞(不可刪除)
           └─ that(可刪除)

簡化從句主語 ─┬─ 保留 ─┬─ 名詞所有格
             │        ├─ 主謂賓補結構
             └─ 刪除 ─┴─ for+n.; 形式主語it

簡化從句謂語 ─┬─ 一般V: -> Ving
             ├─ be+Ving: -> Ving
             ├─ be: -> being
             ├─ be+Ven: -> being+Ven
             ├─ be+n./adj.: -> being+n./adj.
             └─ 情態V: -> to
```

下篇：高階句型─探索修辭變化

四　副詞從句簡化

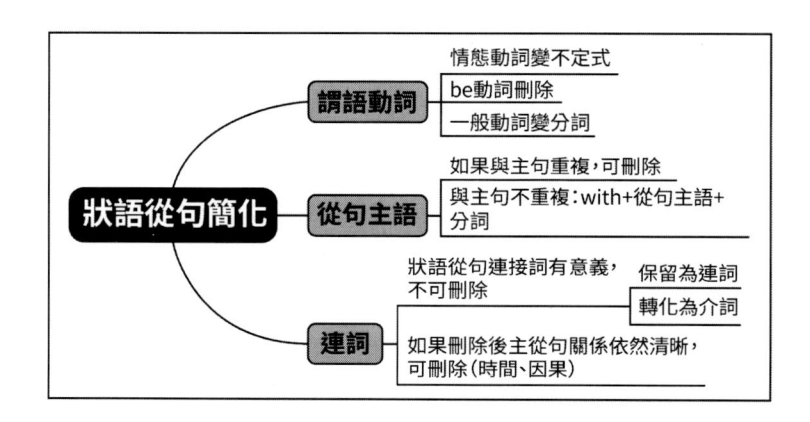

```
                        ┌─ 情態動詞變不定式
            ┌─ 謂語動詞 ─┼─ be動詞刪除
            │           └─ 一般動詞變分詞
            │
            │           ┌─ 如果與主句重複，可刪除
狀語從句簡化 ─┼─ 從句主語 ─┤
            │           └─ 與主句不重複：with+從句主語+分詞
            │
            │           ┌─ 狀語從句連接詞有意義，  ┌─ 保留為連詞
            └─ 連詞 ────┤   不可刪除              └─ 轉化為介詞
                        │
                        └─ 如果刪除後主從句關係依然清晰，
                           可刪除（時間、因果）
```

本節要點提示

- 副詞從句也叫狀語從句。
- 副詞從句的簡化，連接詞是最複雜的環節。
- 副詞從句的主語和從句主語重合時，才能刪除。
- 副詞從句最大程度的簡化，是變成介詞短語。

四　副詞從句簡化

問題1　副詞從句能夠簡化的前提條件是什麼？

＊副詞從句簡化，是從句簡化中最複雜的一種，也是修辭效果最好的一種。而相較於其他從句，副詞從句簡化也需要滿足更多前提條件：

從句主語能刪除，從句才有必要簡化。

主從句主語相同時，從句主語才能刪除。

Because <u>the economy</u> is recovering, <u>people</u> feel hopeful about the future.（主從句主語不同，從句主語不能刪除，從句沒有簡化空間）

＊連接詞不能省略的，從句簡化也沒有意義。

Although the economy is not recovering, people feel hopeful about the future.

➡副詞從句簡化的前提：主從句主語相同，且連接詞可以省略。

~~Because I~~ <u>find</u> a good job, I can support my family now.

簡化為：<u>Finding</u> a good job, I can support my family now.

問題2　從句主語與主句主語不同時，仍要簡化，如何操作？

＊關於「獨立主格」、「分詞構句」的概念剖析。

After <u>my wallet</u> was stolen, <u>the police</u> came and asked many questions.

139

下篇：高階句型—探索修辭變化

簡化為：My wallet stolen, the police came and asked many questions.

➡「with＋從句主語＋分詞」結構

Because he helped us, we found our way back finally.

簡化為：With him helping us, we found our way back finally.

*with 能夠展現的邏輯關係：伴隨或因果。

問題 3　副詞從句的哪些連接詞可以刪除？

*副詞從句有 7 種連接詞，展現主從句間不同的邏輯關係。

(1)時間、地點：before/after/until；

(2)條件：if/as long as/suppose；

(3)因果：as/since/because; so/thus/therefore；

(4)目的：so that/in order that; in case that/lest；

(5)讓步：though/although/while；

(6)限制：as far as/in the sense that；

(7)方式、狀態：as/as if; according to。

*如果刪除連接詞後，主從句間邏輯關係依然清楚，就可以刪除。

四　副詞從句簡化

➡能夠刪除的連接詞類型：時間、因果。

＊同時發生，正在進行

~~While~~ the little girl ~~was~~ watching TV, she heard a strange noise.

簡化為：Watching TV, the little girl heard a strange noise.

＊因果：時間上的先行後續，用句子排列的先後順序展現。

因在前：Because we have no money left, we don't buy anything.

簡化為：Having no money left, we don't buy anything.

果在後：We have no money left, so we don't buy anything.

簡化為：We have no money left, not buying anything.

After+ 先發生的事（從句位置在前，連接詞可刪）：

~~After he was~~ wounded in the working place, he was sent home.

簡化為：Wounded in the working place, he was sent home.

＊省略連接詞後，務必按發生先後排列主從句順序。

He was sent home, wounded in working place.（X）

＊如果有連詞說明上下文關係，就不用要求主從句順序。

He was sent home, after wounded in the working place.

141

下篇：高階句型—探索修辭變化

＊從句動作完成後，主句動作才開始，可以透過分詞的形式變化來展現這種區別。

~~After he~~ wrote the letter, he put it to mail.

簡化為：Writing the letter, he put it to mail.（X）

Having written the letter, he put it to mail.（√）

before+ 後發生的事（從句位置在前，連接詞不可刪）：

~~Before~~ he ~~was~~ in school, he used to be a naughty boy.

簡化為：Before being in school, he used to be a naughty boy.

有時需要變化非謂語動詞形式，來展現多層含義疊加。

Before the house was sold, it belonged to my grandma.（被動）

簡化為：Before being sold, the house belonged to my grandma.

問題 4　副詞從句的哪些連接詞不可以刪除？

7 種連接詞中除因果和時間連詞外的所有情況，有兩種處理方式：

（1）保留連接詞。

Although ~~we~~ have no money left, we can afford everything by credit cards.（讓步狀語從句）

四　副詞從句簡化

可簡化為：Although having no money left, we can afford everything by credit cards.

或添加說明主從句關係的副詞或介詞：

Having no money left, we can still afford everything by credit cards.

* 刪除連接詞後，主從句間邏輯關係發生改變的，就不可刪：

如：方式狀語≠結果狀語

He takes out his credit card, as if he is trying to pay for the shoes.

He takes out his credit card, trying to pay for the shoes.

(2)轉為介詞。

* 把副詞從句簡化為一個含義相同的介詞短語，是最高程度簡化。

As I am an English teacher, I read a lot of English books every day.

變為：分詞結構

Being an English teacher, I read a lot of English books every day.

變為：介詞短語

As an English teacher, I read a lot of English books every day.

下篇：高階句型—探索修辭變化

＊大多數連接詞，都有與之含義接近的介詞或介詞詞組，所以副詞從句幾乎都有可能簡化成介詞短語作狀語。

When he first saw her, he fell in love with her.

簡化為：At the first sight, he fell in love with her.

The outdoor work is delayed, because it is raining.

簡化為：The outdoor work is delayed because of rain.

Although most people opposed the project, it was carried out finally.

簡 化 為：In spite of most people's opposition, the project was carried out finally.

If there should be a fire, the system will send you a message immediately.

簡化為：In case of a fire, the system will send you a message immediately.

問題 5　副詞從句的謂語應如何簡化？

➡與關係從句和名詞從句謂語簡化情況相同：

＊有情態動詞時，變為不定詞。

＊be + 補語，刪除 be，留補語（Ving、Ven、adj.、n.、介詞短語）

* 一般實義動詞或單獨的 be 動詞都在詞尾加 ing 變成現在分詞。

She studies very hard so that ~~she~~ <u>can be</u> admitted to Harvard.

簡化為：She studies very hard <u>to be</u> admitted to Harvard.

I will be very glad <u>if I can help</u> you.

簡化為：I will be very glad <u>to help</u> you.

Although ~~they were~~ <u>killed</u> in the war, they will live in people's hearts forever.

簡化為：Although <u>killed</u> in the war, they will live in people's hearts forever.

Although <u>our company</u> ~~is~~ very small, <u>it</u> is very productive.

簡化為：Although very small, our company is very productive.

~~Because we are~~ with a funny guy, we have a very interesting journey.

簡化為：With a funny guy, we have a very interesting journey.

Before ~~he~~ <u>is</u> a professor, John has been a famous doctor.

簡化為：Before <u>being</u> a professor, John has been a famous doctor.

下篇：高階句型—探索修辭變化

本節內容概要

1. 刪除後不影響上下文邏輯含義的連接詞，才可以刪除，從句簡化的大原則是：不改變原句含義。
2. 刪除 be 動詞，保留補語；情態動詞變不定詞；一般動詞變 Ving 仍是副詞從句簡化的基本方法。
3. 副詞從句最大程度的簡化，是變成邏輯關係一致的介詞短語作狀語。

　＊結合流程圖，總結簡化從句的具體操作要點：

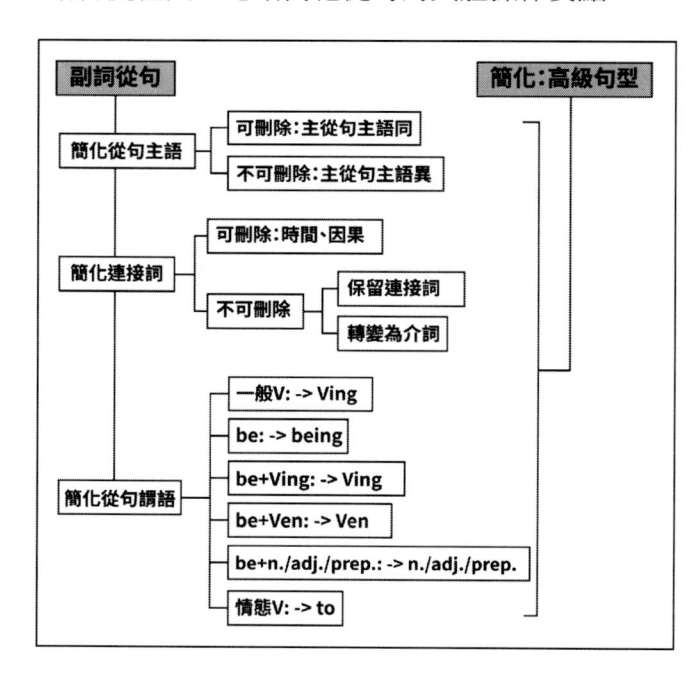

```
副詞從句                                    簡化:高級句型

簡化從句主語 ─┬─ 可刪除:主從句主語同
             └─ 不可刪除:主從句主語異

簡化連接詞 ─┬─ 可刪除:時間、因果
           └─ 不可刪除 ─┬─ 保留連接詞
                       └─ 轉變為介詞

簡化從句謂語 ─┬─ 一般V: -> Ving
             ├─ be: -> being
             ├─ be+Ving: -> Ving
             ├─ be+Ven: -> Ven
             ├─ be+n./adj./prep.: -> n./adj./prep.
             └─ 情態V: -> to
```

五　複句簡化綜合

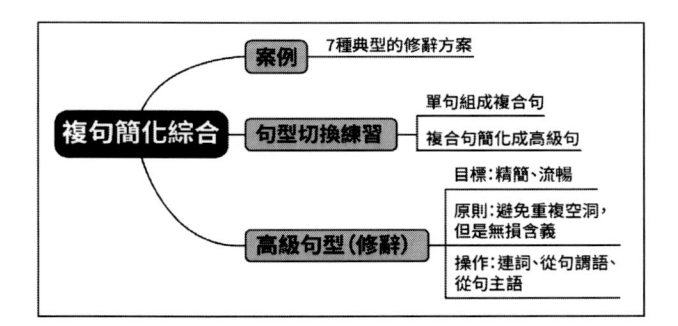

高級句型：綜合運用語法要素和知識的修辭（修辭＝「精」＋「簡」）。

目標：句子精簡流暢。

原則：避免重複空洞；不改變句子原義。

操作：處理連接詞、從句主語、從句謂語。

本節要點提示

- 本節補充7條複句簡化相關的具體實用技巧和注意事項。
- 練習步驟：(1) 組成複句：找各單句的「交叉點」（各小句重複部分），選定一個主句，其他作為從句。 (2) 簡化複句：去除空洞、重複成分。

下篇：高階句型—探索修辭變化

技巧 1　重複謂語➡ as...as 結構。

句 1　I have not practiced very much.

句 2　I should practice very much.

句 3　I am worried about something.（主句）

句 4　I might forget something.

句 5　What should I say during the speech contest?

➡句 1 ＋句 2：I haven't practiced as much as I should.

➡＋句 3：Because I haven't practiced as much as I should, I am worried about something.

簡化為：Not having practiced as much as I should, I am worried about something.

➡＋句 4：I am worried that I might forget something.

簡化為：I am worried about forgetting something.

➡＋句 5：I am worried about forgetting what I should say during the speech contest.

簡化為：I am worried about forgetting what to say during the speech contest.

➡最終簡化結果：Not having practiced as much as I should, I am worried about forgetting what to say during the speech contest.

技巧2　非限定性關係從句。

＊這種從句的缺點是：指代不明，產生歧義；從句最好緊跟先行詞。

＊先行詞是整個句子時，從句簡化成分詞結構，常用於點評事件。

The government invests and builds numerous infrastructures, ~~which~~ <u>accelerates</u> the development of our country.

簡化為：The government invests and builds numerous infrastructures, <u>accelerating</u> the development of our country.

技巧3　名詞所有格之後盡量用單個名詞，而不用名詞詞組。

試比較下面兩種說法：

The audience's <u>not having</u> responded to the question causes awkward silence.

The audience's <u>failure</u> to respond to the question causes awkward silence.

＊名詞所有格之後，表達「沒能做到……」含義，用 failure 更好。

下篇：高階句型—探索修辭變化

技巧 4　「with+n.+ 分詞」結構。

句 1　The summer tourists are all gone.

句 2　The resort town has resumed its air of tranquility. （主句）

➡句 2 作主句，句 1 作原因狀語從句，以連接詞組合：

Now that the summer tourists are all gone, the resort town has resumed its air of tranquility.

簡化為：The summer tourists all gone, the resort town has resumed its air of tranquility.

改為「with+n.+ 分詞」的結構，更口語化的表達：

With the summer tourists all gone, the resort town has resumed its air of tranquility.

技巧 5　兩個含有情態動詞的從句，簡化後可共用一個不定詞符號 to。

句 1　I'd like something.（主句）

句 2　You will meet some people.

句 3　Then you can leave.

➡ 句 1 ＋ 句 2 ＋ 句 3：I'd like that you will meet some people and then you can leave.

簡化：I'd like you to meet some people and then leave.

➡ 進一步改寫：I'd like you to meet some people before leaving.

技巧 6　分詞沒有現在、過去式的分別。

Ving: 進行、主動

Ven: 完成、被動

having+Ven: 發生在前、已經完成

being+Ven: 動名詞的被動式

having been+Ven: 動名詞的被動式，且該動作發生在前已完成

句 1　They are warned not to swim in the pond.

句 2　Something is ineffective.

句 3　They are drowned in the pond.（主句）

➡句 1 ＋句 2：

That they are warned not to swim in the pond is ineffective.

簡化為：Being warned not to swim in the pond is ineffective.

➡＋句 3：Because being warned not to swim in the pond is ineffective, they are drowned in the pond.

151

下篇：高階句型─探索修辭變化

➥引入 have，分清事件的先後順序：

Having been warned not to swim in the pond is ineffective, they are drowned in the pond.

技巧 7　介詞＋名詞／動名詞。

句 1 Bob was the coach of our school football team then.

句 2 Bob saw something.

句 3 Our school football team lost in the important game.

句 4 Bob would assume responsibility.（主句）

句 5 Bob would tender his resignation.

➥句 1 ＋句 4：Bob, who was the coach of our school football team then, would assume responsibility.

簡化為：Bob, the coach of our school football team then, would assume responsibility.

➥句 2 ＋句 3：Bob saw that our school football team lost in the important game.

簡化為：Bob saw our school football team losing in the important game.

簡化為分詞結構：Seeing our school football team losing in the important game,…

五　複句簡化綜合

➡十句 5：Seeing our school football team losing in the important game, Bob, the coach of this team, would assume responsibility by resignation.

本節內容概要

1. 重複謂語，用同等比較結構來解決。
2. 點評整個句子的內容，用逗號＋分詞結構即可。
3. 所有格後用單個名詞更好。
4. 「with+n.+ 分詞」結構更加口語化。
5. 情態動詞未必都要簡化為不定詞。
6. 注意分詞的時間、主被動問題，簡化後句子意思更準確。
7. 介詞後只能接名詞或動名詞，接名詞最自然。

下篇:高階句型—探索修辭變化

六　倒裝句

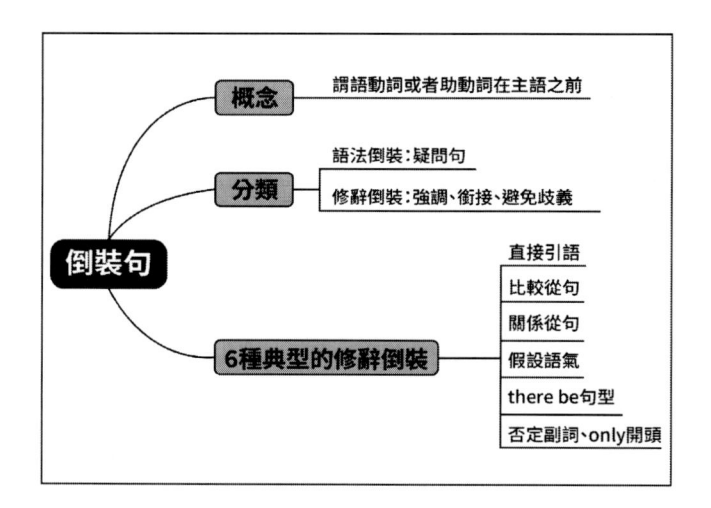

```
倒裝句
├─ 概念 ── 謂語動詞或者助動詞在主語之前
├─ 分類
│    ├─ 語法倒裝:疑問句
│    └─ 修辭倒裝:強調、銜接、避免歧義
└─ 6種典型的修辭倒裝
     ├─ 直接引語
     ├─ 比較從句
     ├─ 關係從句
     ├─ 假設語氣
     ├─ there be句型
     └─ 否定副詞、only開頭
```

本節要點提示

- 語法功能倒裝句最常見的是疑問句;而修辭功能的倒裝句,才是本節的學習重點。主要是一些狀語移至句首表示強調的類型。
- 倒裝句功能:強調;避免重複;避免歧義。

六 倒裝句

問題 1　倒裝句有什麼結構特點？

➡ 一般句型：主語在謂語之前。

➡ 倒裝句：謂語或者助動詞在主語之前；謂語動詞用原形。

＊語法倒裝：疑問句。

＊修辭倒裝的功能：強調；避免重複；避免歧義。

問題 2　修辭倒裝句有哪幾種典型情況？

情況 1：直接引語和間接引語

＊直接引語："You all stay here quietly!" said the boss.

＊間接引語改倒裝句：倒裝是為了強調賓語從句，尤其是從句的主語。

The WHO warns that cholera is coming back.

Cholera, warns the WHO, is coming back.

情況 2：比較從句

＊比較邏輯關係中省略重複內容之後，不倒裝可能產生歧義。

Girls like cats more than boys.

= Girls like cats more than boys do.

下篇：高階句型—探索修辭變化

= Girls like cats more than they like boys.

用倒裝避免歧義：Girls like cats more than do boys.

情況 3：關係從句

* 從句動詞原本搭配的介詞，提到關係詞之前的關係從句才用倒裝：

句 1　The President is a man.（主句）

句 2　A heavy responsibility falls on the President.

➡ 句 2 ＋ 句 1：The President is a man whom a heavy responsibility falls on.

The President is a man on whom a heavy responsibility falls.

倒　裝：The President is a man on whom falls a heavy responsibility.

* 如果關係從句前沒有介詞，或者關係詞作主語，就不用倒裝：

The President is a man who bears a heavy responsibility.

情況 4：假設語氣

* 謂語部分含有 be 動詞或助動詞的 if 條件從句，可以省略 if，把 be 動詞或助動詞提到主語前，構成假設效果：

If I had arrived home earlier, I could have met uncle Sam.

倒　裝：Had I arrived home earlier, I could have met uncle Sam.

情況 5：there be 句型

＊包括一切以地點狀語開頭的句子，動詞也不限於 be 動詞；

there be 和 here be 句型是最典型的情況。

功能：強調地點狀語。

倒裝：動詞提前，與句首的地點狀語相連，位置在主語之前。

There goes the train.（＝The train goes there.）

Here is your ticket.（＝Your ticket is here.）

On the riverbank lies my hometown.（＝My hometown lies on the riverbank.）

情況 6：否定副詞或者 only 開頭的句子

＊否定副詞 not、never、hardly、barely、rarely、scarcely、seldom 等，以及語氣副詞 only，放在句子開頭，來加強語氣時，句子會出現倒裝。

＊倒裝的原因：強調＋銜接。狀語前置以強調，謂語和狀語關係密切，所以置換到主語前，以接近狀語。

We don't have such luck every day.

下篇：高階句型—探索修辭變化

倒裝：Not every day do we have such luck.

*not 和 until 引導的整個時間狀語從句提前，可以表示強調：

We will not stop supplying food until you complete the task.

倒裝：Not until you complete the task will we stop supplying food.

* 如果否定詞修飾主語，本來就在句子開頭，句子不用倒裝：

倒裝：Hardly have I ever heard about this.

不倒裝：Hardly anyone has ever heard about this.

*only 的情況與否定副詞相同：I met him only yesterday.

only 提前表強調，要倒裝：Only yesterday did I meet him.

only 修飾主語，不用倒裝：Only I met him yesterday.

* 注意：not only...but also 結構，連接的是對等成分，倒裝時要兼顧對等成分的對仗工整。

He not only passed the test but also scored at the top.

（not only 修飾 passed；but also 修飾 scored）

not only 移至句首表示強調，構成倒裝：

Not only did he pass the test, but he also scored at the top.

（not only 修飾一個句子；but also 也要修飾一個句子）

六　倒裝句

情況 7：其他情況 —— 常用的簡短倒裝句。

Jack is an engineer. <u>So</u> am I.

<u>Long</u> live the King!

問題 3　句子為什麼需要倒裝？

➡句子成分提前是為了強調，順序調整是為了把關係更密切的內容連接在一起，讓句子更清楚、流暢。

本節內容概要

可能出現句子倒裝的 6 種情況分別是：

1. 直接引語。
2. 比較從句。
3. 介詞＋關係詞引導的關係從句。
4. 省略 if 的假設條件句。
5. 狀語開頭，強調地點的句子。
6. 否定副詞或 only 開頭的句子。

下篇：高階句型—探索修辭變化

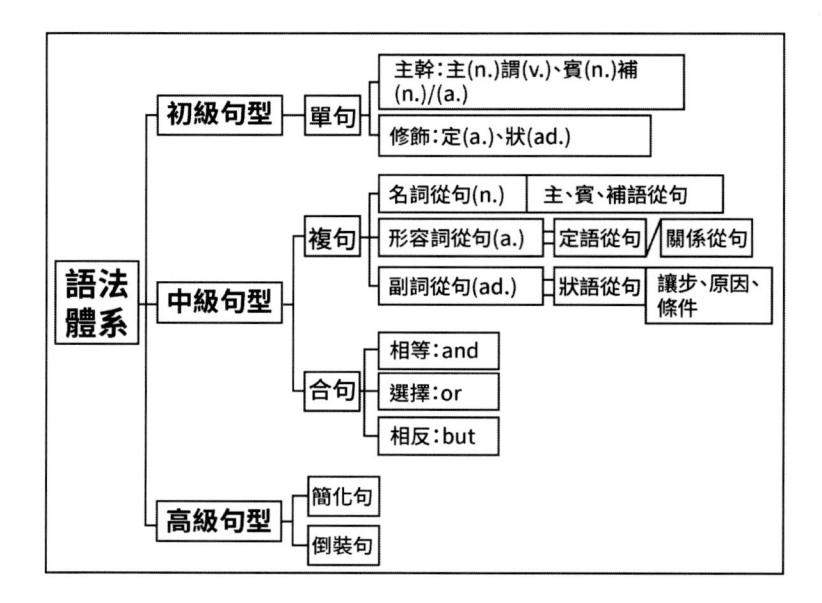

```
                              ┌─ 主幹：主(n.)謂(v.)、賓(n.)補
              ┌─ 初級句型 ─ 單句 ─┤      (n.)/(a.)
              │                └─ 修飾：定(a.)、狀(ad.)
              │
              │              ┌─ 名詞從句(n.) ─ 主、賓、補語從句
              │              │
              │        ┌─ 複句 ─ 形容詞從句(a.) ─ 定語從句 / 關係從句
              │        │     │
              │        │     └─ 副詞從句(ad.) ─ 狀語從句 ─ 讓步、原因、
語法                   │                                   條件
體系 ─┼─ 中級句型 ─┤
              │        │     ┌─ 相等：and
              │        │     │
              │        └─ 合句 ─ 選擇：or
              │              │
              │              └─ 相反：but
              │
              │              ┌─ 簡化句
              └─ 高級句型 ─┤
                            └─ 倒裝句
```

參考書目

英文

［1］ WADDELL L A. The Aryan Origin of the Alphabet ——Disclosing the Sumero-Phoenician Parentage of our Letters Ancient and Modern ［M］. Literary Licensing, LLC. 2013.

［2］ SACKS D. Letter Perfect: The Marvelous History of Our Alphabet From A to Z ［M］. Broadway, 2004.

［3］ LINDSTROMBERG S. English Prepositions Explained ［M］. John Benjamins Publishing Company, 2010.

［4］ PARTRIDGE E, Origins. A Short Etymological Dictionary of Modern English ［M］. Routledge, 2008.

［5］ DEVLIN J. How to Speak and Write Correctly ［M］. Arc Manor, 2007.

［6］ SWINTON W. New Word Analysis or School Etymology of English Derivative Words ［M］. BiblioLife, 2009.

［7］ DOUSE, Thomas Le Marchant. Grimm's Law ［M］. BiblioLife, 2008.

［8］ LEWIS N. Word Power Made Easy ［M］. Anchor, 2014.

參考書目

中文

[1] 諾姆‧喬姆斯基。句法結構［M］（黃長著譯）。北京：中國社會科學出版社，1979.

[2] 約瑟夫‧皮爾西。英語的故事［M］（賀京平譯）。北京：中國友誼出版社，2017.

[3] 陸國強。現代英語辭彙學［M］‧上海：上海外語教育出版社，1999.

[4] 陸國強。英漢概念結構對比［M］‧上海：上海外語教育出版社，2008.

[5] 陸國強。思維模式與翻譯［M］‧上海：上海外語教育出版社，2012.

[6] 陸國強。漢譯英常用表達式經典慣例［M］‧上海：上海外語教育出版社，2012.

[7] L. G. 亞歷山大。朗文英語語法［M］‧北京：外語教學與研究出版社，1991.

[8] 張滿勝。英語語法新思維［M］‧北京：世界知識出版社，2000.

[9] 旋元佑。英語魔法師之語法俱樂部［M］‧北京：九州出版社，2001.

[10] 張道真。張道真實用英語語法［M］‧北京：外語教學與研究出版社，2002.

國家圖書館出版品預行編目資料

英語語法──從單字到句子：不怕開口說英語！用語法搭建橋梁，解決溝通難題 / 楊篁璐 著 . -- 第一版 . -- 臺北市 : 財經錢線文化事業有限公司，2025.01
面； 公分
POD 版
ISBN 978-626-408-131-3(平裝)
1.CST: 英語 2.CST: 語法
805.16　　　　　　　113020281

電子書購買

爽讀 APP

臉書

英語語法──從單字到句子：不怕開口說英語！用語法搭建橋梁，解決溝通難題

作　　　者：楊篁璐
發　行　人：黃振庭
出　版　者：財經錢線文化事業有限公司
發　行　者：崧燁文化事業有限公司
E - m a i l：sonbookservice@gmail.com
粉　絲　頁：https://www.facebook.com/sonbookss/
網　　　址：https://sonbook.net/
地　　　址：台北市中正區重慶南路一段 61 號 8 樓
8F., No.61, Sec. 1, Chongqing S. Rd., Zhongzheng Dist., Taipei City 100, Taiwan
電　　　話：(02) 2370-3310　傳真：(02) 2388-1990
印　　　刷：京峯數位服務有限公司
律師顧問：廣華律師事務所 張珮琦律師

-版權聲明-
本書版權為中國經濟出版社所有授權財經錢線文化事業有限公司獨家發行電子書及繁體書繁體字版。若有其他相關權利及授權需求請與本公司聯繫。
未經書面許可，不得複製、發行。

定　　　價：299 元
發行日期：2025 年 01 月第一版
◎本書以 POD 印製